A PRIZE WORTH FIGHTING FOR

THIEVES OF DESIRE

BOOK THREE

ELLIE ST. CLAIR

CONTENTS

Facebook: Ellie St. Clair

Cover by AJF Designs

Do you love historical romance? Receive access to a free ebook, as well as exclusive content such as giveaways, contests, freebies and advance notice of pre-orders through my mailing list!

Sign up here!

Also By Ellie St. Clair

Thieves of Desire
The Art of Stealing a Duke's Heart
A Jewel for the Taking
A Prize Worth Fighting For
Gambling for the Lost Lord's Love
Romance of a Robbery

Thieves of Desire Box Set

For a full list of all of Ellie's books, please see www.elliestclair.com/books.

CHAPTER 1

LONDON ~ 1814

He wasn't going to fit.

Damien shifted this way and that as he tried to miraculously shrink so that he could squeeze himself inside.

But he was out of luck.

He sighed as he lifted his head and gave up, hoping that, at the very least, his embarrassment hadn't caught the attention of anyone else in the room.

He was sorely mistaken.

For a moment — just one moment — he caught the smile of a woman as she watched him, before she dipped her head and hurried away, no longer visible behind the marble post of the bookshop's reading room.

He scratched his forehead as he took the small book in his meaty palm and rounded the corner created by the multitudes of high-rising bookshelves, hiding deeper in the recesses of the room behind another of the white marble pillars.

Damien's usual seat was, unfortunately, occupied, which meant that if he didn't find what he was looking for, he would have to abandon his quest for peace today. This was the only place he could find it. Well, not this building, exactly, but what the building offered him. Books. Stories. Adventure.

He certainly couldn't lose himself in such literature at home.

His family may all have been well educated considering their upbringing — his eldest brother and father figure, Arie, had seen to that — but that didn't mean that any of them spent their *leisure* time in such pursuits.

No, education was for one purpose only — to prepare them for the work that would be required of them as part of the Hondros family.

Damien lumbered over to the far corner, finally finding a sofa that would accommodate his wide girth. He settled in, propped up his feet, and lost himself in Captain Jack for the rest of the afternoon.

Some prepared for battle by envisioning the fight to come. Others warmed up their bodies, putting themselves through the motions of the fight. Still others physically prepared themselves to look the part.

But not Damien. Damien chose, instead, to forget everything that he was going to have to do, and live the life of someone else instead.

Tonight… tonight he would become the warrior he had been trained to be.

For now, he would take solace in the only time he could truly be himself.

* * *

GRACE FORCED herself not to stare.

A man like him, so striking, so imposing, would never take a second look at a woman like her, so why even bother trying?

But she couldn't help herself from peeking around the corner, spying on him as he relaxed into the sofa and opened the book in his thick hands. He had caught her watching him once already — she didn't want him to notice again.

"Are you watching him again?"

Grace jumped before turning to her friend, Lydia, who sat next to her with one eyebrow raised knowingly.

"I'm not watching anyone in particular," she said, attempting nonchalance. "I am simply perusing the room."

"Mmm hmm," Lydia said, making it clear she didn't believe anything Grace had said. "Which is why you have insisted that we visit at the exact same time every Friday, when a certain man just happens to be here, one who you cannot take your eyes off of?"

"I—" Grace began to try to defend herself, but heat flooded her face. She had never been particularly adept at lying, and Lydia had known her for far too many years to be easily fooled. "I find him…" she paused, unable to put into words exactly what it was about this man that drew him to her in such a way. "Different."

"Different." Lydia snorted before rolling her eyes at Grace. "I love you, but I shall never understand you."

"You wouldn't be the first," Grace said with a small smile. Her family most certainly never had. Her father owned a shipping company, and her three brothers had all found roles for themselves within the business in one way or the other. She, the youngest, was the only one who didn't have a purpose, who found herself lost unless she had her nose within the pages of a book, where she could take on the thoughts and feelings of someone else entirely.

"Why don't you go talk to him?" Lydia asked, crossing one leg over the other as she leaned back in her seat. They were currently ensconced in the corner of the bookshop's reading room. Grace was trying to decide which of the four new novels she wished to take home with her, although truth be told she would likely finish at least one each day so she might as well pack them all up. Perhaps Mr. Moon would allow her an extra two.

"*Talk* to him?" Grace said, her mouth opening in a round O of horror. "I could never."

"Why not?" Lydia said with a shrug, tucking one of her reddish curls back into her bonnet. Grace had always envied the magnificent hue, when her own dark blond locks were forever escaping their pins to fall limply around her shoulders. "It isn't as though he is some fancy lord. He couldn't be — not a man of his size, nor with knuckles so bruised."

Grace followed Lydia's words to the man's hands. She had noticed how large they were but hadn't seen the scrapes upon them. Lydia, ever observant, was absolutely right. Grace's heart fell as she began to wonder how he had ever come by such marks.

"I have no wish to speak to him," Grace said, shifting in her seat so that he was no longer in her line of vision, attempting to prove the truth of her words to Lydia. "I am here to spend a lovely afternoon with you and to borrow new books to bring joy to my week. That is all."

"Very well," Lydia said, as she returned her own stack of books. "If you say so."

Grace nodded. She did. For there was one thing she had to remind herself. She would never be one of the heroines in her stories. And the more she remembered that, the better off and less disappointed she would be.

* * *

DAMIEN LET OUT a sigh of contentment as he finished the book and placed it down on the small table beside him. It had taken three visits to finish, but the three visits were well worth it. Now, what was it he had to do?

He rubbed at his forehead as he pulled his old pocket watch out of his jacket, rubbing the scuff marks as though he could erase them before peering through them at the time.

A quarter to five. Which meant he had been here—a quarter to five! He jumped up, his heart beating fast. He was supposed to be at the ring by six. He should have been home to meet Arie by at least four o'clock. His brother was not going to be pleased, and Damien could only hope that he would still allow the fight to go forward. He began to rush out the door, belatedly remembering his book. He picked it up before rushing across the room, practically throwing it across the desk of Mr. Moon, the clerk, with a hushed "thanks" as he went by. His speed caused the door to fly forward, hitting a gentleman who stumbled ahead, upsetting a cart that had been parked nearby. The cart began to roll down the street, right into the path of an oncoming carriage. The startled horse reared up and pawed at the air, ready to come crashing down on a woman standing beside him.

It all happened so fast that had Damien been anyone else, he likely would have been able to do nothing but watch in horror as the woman was trampled.

But, despite his size, Damien had reflexes quicker than most. He didn't even think. Instead, he rushed across the sidewalk, not caring who he pushed out of his way in order to reach the other side. Somehow, he wasn't sure how, he made it to her in time, wrapping his body around hers as he fell with her to the side, cushioning her from the ground as they rolled upon it.

Then, as much as time had slowed while he rushed toward her, it suddenly all began to move ahead once more and Damien realized where he was and what he was doing — lying on top of a woman he had never met before in the midst of dozens of onlookers on Piccadilly Street, books strewn around them as though a book cart had been upended.

When he looked down at the woman to ask her if she was all right, however, suddenly none of that mattered. For his gaze caught hers, and she was staring up at him with such supplication that he couldn't turn his head away from those brown eyes that had caught him in their stare.

"Thank you," she practically breathed, her eyes glistening. "You saved my life."

"I… I did no such thing," he mumbled as he became all too aware of her plush body beneath his. Most women were so small, so fragile that he thought he would break them even if he barely touched them. Not this woman. She was built as a woman should be built — all luscious curves that he could sink into and lose himself in.

He scrambled backward before she elicited further reaction from him, reaching a hand down to help her up. She placed her hand, enclosed in a practical leather glove, into his, allowing him to assist her. The two of them stared at one another for a moment before looking around them and then noticing the books strewn all over the ground. She broke the stare to look around them.

"The books will be ruined!" she exclaimed in horror.

They crouched at the same time, softly bumping their heads into one another as they did so.

"I'm so sorry," he said, knowing that it must have hurt her much more than it ever would him with his thick skull.

"Not at all," she said somewhat shyly, raising a hand to readjust her bonnet and he realized she was the woman who had been watching him in the bookshop. "Between my hat and the layers of hair beneath, I barely felt it."

"It's not just that," he said gruffly as he placed the books into her outstretched arms and the two of them stood. "It was my fault you were in such a predicament in the first place. I—"

"Nearly had my friend killed!" said a glowering woman he hadn't noticed until now. She was as thin as the first woman was buxom, the nose she held in the air as she looked at him somewhat hooked. "I saw the entire thing."

"Yes, you are correct, Miss," he said, dipping his head. "It was my fault. I hope you are well and I am so sorry again." Suddenly church bells began to chime in the distance, and he cursed, remembering the time. "I must go. Farewell."

Before he could spend another moment caught in this woman's spell as he had been in his book, he turned and began to run down the street.

* * *

"Well, I never," Lydia said, crossing her arms as the two of them watched the mystery man run down the street with surprising quickness for a man of his size. "Who does he think he is?"

"I don't know," Grace mused, unable to tear her eyes from him. "But I'd rather like to find out."

"Grace Mulberry!" Lydia said, placing her hands on her hips now as she turned to look at her, and it was now Grace's turn to roll her eyes. She might not have a friend better than Lydia, but she had also never met anyone quite so judgemental. "That man came rushing out of the bookshop with such little regard for everyone around him that he nearly killed you in the process."

"But he saved me," Grace protested as they began down the street toward Grace's home on the outskirts of Holborn.

"Because he had no choice," Lydia insisted. "I do hope you

aren't getting any romantic notions into your head, Grace. You don't even know the man's name or have any idea who he is."

"No," she agreed. "But nor did I earlier today, before I met him."

"You didn't meet him."

"I suppose you're right," Grace said, but her earlier hesitancy had fled, to be replaced by something else — determination. "But that doesn't mean I can't discover who he is."

"And just how are you going to do that?" Lydia asked.

"I have my ways."

"You're going to wait at that bookshop until he returns, aren't you?"

"Something like that."

"Oh, Grace," Lydia said, raising her face heavenward as though God would have the answer for her. "Just what am I going to do with you?"

CHAPTER 2

Arie had been about as displeased as Damien had imagined him to be.

"Are you aware of the time?" Arie asked as Damien burst through the door, still at a run as he raced by him and up the stairs to his room. "You should have been home hours ago."

"I know!" Damien called down, even as he heard Arie's tread on the stairs. He opened the door to Damien's bedroom, uncaring that Damien was halfway undressed.

"You're not going to be able to eat in time."

"I know."

"You won't be prepared."

"I will."

"You better not embarrass us."

"Never have. Won't start now."

"Very well," Arie said. "We'll leave when you're ready."

Arie dismissed him, but Damien soon sensed another presence fill the doorway, and he lifted his head for a moment to find his other brother, Xander, watching him.

"What are you doing here?" Damien asked, although he

was grateful to see him. The two of them had become particularly close over the past couple of years, and he missed living in the same house was his brother. Thankfully, Xander and his wife, Juliet, weren't far.

"I came to support you," Xander said, propping his lean frame up against the doorway. "Looks like you need it. Can I help?"

"Sure," Damien said, and Xander strolled into the room, lifting the pieces of clothing off the bed and helping Damien dress.

Xander said nothing as they worked in concert in the same way they had far too many times before.

"Who are you fighting tonight?" Xander finally asked, breaking the silence.

"Joe Conrad."

"Ah, good old Joe," Xander said, slapping Damien on the shoulder after he helped him into his shirt, which Damien would shed once they reached the ring beneath the gaming hell Arie conveniently owned. "Do the two of you still spar?"

"We do," Damien confirmed, already somewhat ill at ease with the thought of fighting his friend that evening. "Had a lot to rehearse for tonight."

"Of course," Xander murmured, and Damien wondered whether he might have caught a hint of judgement in Xander's tone. But how could he judge Damien for anything after his own involvement in a fair amount of the family's schemes past, present, and future?

"Who is to be the victor tonight?" Xander asked, coming around in front of Damien to help him wrap his hands. Damien preferred to ready himself as much as he could before arriving, where the noise of the crowd threatened to distract him.

"Me," Damien said bluntly. "Arie feels that our… authority

in St. Giles has lessened somewhat as of late, so he'd like to remind everyone of just why the Hondros family is not one to question. That anyone who might take any issue with us or think to question us should think twice."

"Ah, using you to scare people away," Xander said, eyeing him knowingly as he pushed back some of his far-too-long dark hair. "If only they knew."

Damien snorted as he shrugged into his jacket. "Right."

"No offence at that. Just meaning that you are one of the gentlest men I know. Not to mention the member of this family who prevents the rest of us from killing one another."

"Now *that* is the truth," Damien said with a wry grin. "The rest of you would never have lasted together so long without me."

Xander, normally the one wearing the notoriously ever-present affable grin, suddenly sobered as he studied Damien. "He doesn't appreciate you as he should, you know," he said gruffly.

"What do you mean?" Damien asked, even though he knew exactly what Xander was getting at.

"Arie. He uses you for your muscle, tries to make you into this formidable fighter of a man when your true nature is anything but. Why do you even still do this?"

"Why not?" Damien said with a shrug. "What else is there to do?"

"I don't know, perhaps find a different way to live? Help Arie with something other than planting your fist in someone's face or taking one in the nose? Soon that pretty mug of yours is going to be entirely ruined."

Even while Damien's stomach churned as Xander's words took root, he barked out a laugh. "My face has never been a pretty one and you know it."

"Doesn't seem to make much difference to the ladies. It's

funny, I was the one all thought to be the rake and charmer, when it was you who was always going home with someone new."

Damien shook his head with a smirk. "Only because you were pining after Juliet."

"Perhaps," Xander shrugged. "But that doesn't change the fact that, pretty face or not, women seem to like a man who can protect them. Maybe one of these days you'll find one you enjoy and settle down. It's not so bad, you know."

That sobered Damien. "I haven't found anyone I think I can stand for more than a night. Besides, I'm not sure I even *want* to bring a woman into this life, Xander. You should understand that better than anyone."

Xander had nearly lost Juliet for that very reason — he'd been trying to protect her from himself, his family, and their ways. As it turned out, however, they were far better off together, no matter what they faced. But there weren't many Juliets — most women had no wish nor any of the sense necessary to survive long in the world Damien and his family inhabited. But he didn't want to get into that with his brother. Not right now. He had other things with which to concern himself.

"I understand," Xander said, although the expression in his odd indigo eyes seemed grave as his gaze roved over Damien. "I just want you to be as happy as I am."

"Don't worry about me, brother," Damien said, clapping Xander on the shoulder, surprised by the gratefulness flooding through him that this man, who may not have been his brother by blood but was so in every other way, would always be there for him. "I'm happy as I am."

He managed a smile before crossing to the door, knowing that Arie would be downstairs pacing, afraid that his carefully planned bout tonight would go to shit due to Damien's tardiness.

He was just about to pull the door open when Xander called out to him once more.

"One last thing."

"Yes?"

"You don't *have* to do this anymore, Damien. Not if you don't want to."

"That's the thing, Xander," he said, turning back around to look out the door, needing to hide the pain that might make itself evident on his face. "I don't have a choice."

* * *

"I WOULD HAVE FAR PREFERRED to stay home tonight," Grace said with a sigh as she settled into her seat beside her brother.

"Father has money on the fight," Borden said. "He wants us all in attendance to see him win big."

"Of course he does," she said, rolling her eyes.

She hadn't often attended fights, but her father liked to make a showing of his family — of how far he had come from his humble beginnings in St. Giles; how he had built himself from nothing to become one of the wealthiest merchants in London. She was aware that he was not known as the most… scrupulous businessman, but he didn't seem to care, as long as he had the wealth that accompanied his endeavors.

"Sit up straight, Grace Ellen," her father said from her other side. "You don't know who might be watching. And don't roll your eyes at me."

While appearances were of the utmost importance to her father, she was aware that he did love his children, despite his sternness. He tapped his own chin as a reminder to tell her to lift hers, and she sighed but did as he bid.

"I thought he had moved onto horses," she whispered to her brother Bordon, who grinned at her remark.

"He did," their brother, Jeremiah said, leaning forward, his voice equally low as he turned to her, "but he can't resist when Damien Hondros is fighting."

"Damien Hondros?" she echoed, confused by the strange surname.

"You know who he is — you must. Everyone knows the Hondros family," Bordon said, his eyebrows forming a V as he looked at her.

Grace shrugged. She had never been particularly proficient with names and preferred to stay as uninvolved as possible from any of her father's business dealings.

"Well, anyway, Hondros is one of the younger brothers. There haven't been many fights that he hasn't won. But Father heard that tonight might be a different outcome. That the Hondros family isn't as powerful as they once were and Damien shouldn't be as feared as he used to be."

Grace nodded absently, her mind already wandering to which of her newly borrowed books she might begin after this fight. While her father enjoyed showing off his wealth when he was in public, he was always after Grace for burning candles well into the night as she lay awake unable to sleep until she turned the last page.

Her only hope was that this match would be over sooner rather than later.

And that her father came away with his winnings. For if he didn't, there would be grumbling for days, and someone — never himself, of course — would be receiving the blame.

A man walked out into the middle of the ring, greeting the crowd and announcing the feature match to come. The throng began to cheer wildly, but then he brought to the ring two other men that apparently no one had ever heard of before, for a few boos echoed throughout the crowd. Grace sighed. She didn't overly care about the fighters, but her back was already sore from the hard planks of the bench beneath and behind her, and an additional match meant more time she had to sit through all of this.

Fortunately, it didn't take long for one of the men to be knocked out, and the main event began.

Grace closed her eyes, wondering if she could, perhaps, take a nap during the fight, which could mean more time to read later that evening.

But then one sickening crunch had her wincing, and while she had squeezed her eyes tight, she couldn't help opening one eye slightly to see what had happened.

Her eyes flew open as he gasped so loudly that both her father and Borden turned to see what was the matter.

But she had no explanation. What was she supposed to say? That the man in front of her, delivering one blow after another into the body of a man equally as large and ferocious, was the same man who had sat in the library, his eyes running over the pages of a book for hours? Who had rescued her, and held her in his arms so gently, whose eyes hadn't left her until he ensured she was fine?

Perhaps her eyes were deceiving her. For while the facial features were familiar, this brute, whose face had hardened into a ruthless scowl, could not be the same gentle, kind man from earlier, the man that she had been so captivated by. Grace hated violence. She didn't even like seeing her brothers get into a fistfight when they disagreed upon something.

Could he have a twin? Or was it another man who just looked similar?

The fighter — Damien, Bordon had called him — circled around his opponent, and when he did, his face was directly in her line of vision. It was him. It had to be.

All of her suspicions were confirmed when he looked up as though he could feel her watching him, and met her gaze.

He stopped, stilled, stood there staring — until his opponent's fist caught him right in the nose and he went down with a sickening thud.

CHAPTER 3

"Damien! Get up, man! Up!"

Damien blinked rapidly and shook his head from side to side as the blackness cleared and the roaring of the crowd filled his ears.

What had happened? He and Joe had been boxing — he caught his friend now looking down at him with concern on his features — and something had happened. But what?

Oh yes. Her face flooded back into his mind, and he closed his eyes briefly as he remembered. *She* was here. But why?

"Damien — up, *now*!"

It was no longer the voice of his trainer, Ivan, that filled his head, but Arie. His brother had approached the ring, his normally placid if somewhat devious expression now enraged as he looked down at his brother.

Damien dimly shook away the last of the fog that hung around his head and flipped himself over onto his hands and knees. A break was called in the fight, and he half-crept, half-shuffled toward Ivan who was awaiting him in the corner.

"Are you all right? What happened out there?" Ivan

demanded, but there was no way for Damien to tell him that he had seen some mystery woman in the crowd who he had briefly met for five minutes earlier that day after nearly killing her.

"I'm fine," Damien said, his tongue feeling thick until Ivan held out a container of water, and he splashed it over his face and into his mouth. "I'll get back out there and finish the job."

"See that you do," Ivan said, slapping him on the shoulder, "or Arie will have something to say about it."

Damien stood and jumped up and down on the balls of his feet a couple of times as he tried to send life back through his body. *Focus, Damien. Focus. Forget her.*

Had he not told Xander just shortly before that he had no time for women? He had hardly thought her remarkable when he had seen her in the library. But there was something about her — something that called to him for reasons he couldn't properly express.

And now she was here.

As for why, he would have to worry about that later. For right now, he had a match to finish. He punched one fist into the palm of his other hand and stepped toward Joe. They nodded at one another grimly. Time to finish this.

DAMIEN RUBBED at his forehead as he sat back in the wooden chair that was nearly as battered as he was while Ivan held a cold, damp piece of linen to the cuts and bruises that were already beginning to form over his face and body. Ivan was silent, his grim expression saying far more than any words ever could. They both knew that Arie was about to say enough.

"Damien!"

The door opened with a bang and Damien groaned at the

entrance as well as the sting of his cuts, aware that his brief reprieve after the match was now complete.

"Finished paying out the winnings?" Damien asked wryly, holding out a bruised, swollen hand. "I'm ready for my own cut."

"Enough," Arie said, crossing his arms over his chest. "What was that out there?"

"Well," Damien said slowly, not wanting to anger Arie any further but also finished with taking all of his berating when he was doing nothing but sacrificing his body and honor for his brother and their family, "I would call that boxing in a match. A fixed match, true, but a match nonetheless. I won, Arie, so I don't understand what the issue is."

"The issue?" A vein in Arie's forehead bulged, a sure sign of his anger. "The *issue* is the way you bungled that one which made it quite clear that your win was obviously orchestrated. Joe could have beaten you a thousand different ways while you stood there, mooning at whatever caught your attention in the crowd. What, did a pretty face catch your eye? You should know better than that, that you should be saving your wandering eye for *after* the match. It's your brother who mixes business with his own pleasure, not you."

Damien stood at that. He could handle Arie making comments about him and his wandering attention. But he was finished with hearing Arie's pointed remarks about Xander and his wife. They had made their amends, and Arie had never said anything further to Xander's face, but he still made the odd sly comment behind his back. Damien was finished with it.

"Xander gave up everything for you and has spent most of his life doing nothing but trying to make you happy," Damien said, advancing on Arie, whose eyes widened in surprise, and rightly so. Arie had rescued Damien when he was but a year old, bringing him with him onto the shores of

England and providing for him ever since. Damien wouldn't be alive if it wasn't for Arie — and they both knew it, which was why Damien usually didn't respond to his brother. Damien took a breath, calming somewhat when he saw the hurt seep into Arie's eyes. "I'm sorry I lost focus. It won't happen again. But I won, Arie, so I don't understand the issue."

"You won because of Joe," Arie said. "If it wasn't for him—"

"Arie Hondros!" came a bellowing from the other side of the door, as what must be either a very large and meaty or very angry fist banged against it. "I need to talk to you, and I need to talk to you now!"

Arie raised an I-told-you-so eyebrow at Damien as he strode over to the door, setting his shoulders before reaching for the knob. He might not have been as big as Damien, but when he wanted to, he could certainly be as imposing, and always far more dangerous.

He opened the door, although he did not step back to allow anyone entrance.

Damien took a side step so that he could see who dared to challenge Arie, glimpsing a red-faced middle-aged man, a hat askew on his bald head, raising a pointed finger at Arie.

"You owe me five hundred pounds!" he shouted, and Arie tilted his head in that calm way that was always so aggravating when one was upset with him.

"Oh?" Arie said. "Care to explain why, Mulberry?"

Mulberry… Damien allowed the name to roll around his already bruised brain. Where did he know that name? He knew he was a man of some importance, although he couldn't say just exactly why.

"Because that match was thrown!"

"I can assure you that my brother would never take part in a thrown match, Mulberry," Arie said icily. "If you chose to bet against him — something I would never advise — that is your own fault."

"I saw it, as did everyone in those stands," Mulberry sneered as he leaned in toward him. "The match should have been over as soon as your brother was on the ground, but instead Conrad allowed him to have at him. Might as well have hung a bag of sand in the air. I won't have it!"

"Get out of here, Mulberry, before I decide that neither you nor your money are ever welcome in this establishment again," Arie said from between clenched teeth.

Damien ran a hand over his forehead. He was finished with this — for tonight at least. He just wanted to get out of here, to have a hot meal and climb into bed where he could sleep away the dull ache that pounded through his skull.

He crossed the room, taking the door from Arie's grasp and opening it wider, adopting his most ferocious scowl.

"Listen here, Mulberry, if my brother has asked you to leave, then I suggest—"

He stopped abruptly, suddenly forgetting everything he was going to say.

For behind Mulberry, lining the corridor beyond, were two young men and a woman that could only be the man's offspring, for they all so looked alike.

And the woman was the one who, unbeknownst to her, had caused this whole disaster.

She was now looking at him with nothing but distaste.

* * *

He was staring at her. Why was he staring at her — again?

Because, you dolt, he recognizes you as the woman who almost got herself trampled by a stampeding horse and is now here at his boxing match like some sort of lurker.

He likely thought she was following him. And he

wouldn't be far from the truth. Except, as it turned out, Lydia was right. Grace had imagined him as someone else entirely, had fictionalized him into one of the heroes of her books. He was nothing like the gentle giant of a man she had thought him to be, but was instead the most violent man she had ever encountered.

"You suggest what, Hondros?" her father said, doing what he always did and finding a gap in the man's armor. "For I'm no Joe Conrad, who's going to let you throw me around for payday."

"Enough."

The one word from the man — Arie Hondros, according to her father — cut through the tension in the air.

"I mean it, Mulberry. You will take your accusations and your offspring and get out of my face before you say something that will have much more dire consequences than the loss of money that you so irresponsibly gambled away. Do you understand me?"

Grace sucked in a breath. This wasn't going to go well. She had seen her father so challenged before, and it had ended badly. She braced herself for the outburst to follow, wishing that they could be gone from here much more quickly — but then her father surprised her.

"Very well," he said in a considerably calmer voice. "But we are not finished here. Not by a longshot."

At that he turned, flicking his hand forward. "Come, let's go."

"But, Father—" her brother Jeremiah began, but their father gave a nearly imperceptible shake of his head that told them now was not the time to argue. They fell into line behind him, and Grace couldn't help herself from looking back over her shoulder — just once — to see *him* again. He might not be the man she thought he was, but that didn't mean her imaginings had to be ruined.

They had just rounded the corner of the corridor when Grace felt the tug on her sleeve. She whirled around to find him — Damien Hondros — standing there awkwardly, shuffling back and forth from one foot to the other.

"Can I speak to you for a moment?"

Grace hesitated. She should say no. Her father and brothers were likely already halfway out the building. She peeked around the corner, seeing Borden waiting for her.

"I'll be there in one moment, all right?" she said, and he looked at her with suspicion, but then nodded his head. Her brothers were protective, but they had always given her freedom to do as she pleased.

She turned back, squaring her shoulders as she summoned all of the courage within her to face him. This was not like her. Not at all. She was not a woman who met strange men in corridors beside a boxing ring in the underground of a gaming hell. Had her father not been so irate, even he would never have brought her down here. But here she was.

"Yes?" she said, unsure of why he would want to speak with her. They knew nothing of one another, besides the brief moment of their chance encounter earlier that very day.

"I just…" He scratched the side of his head, seeming surprised when he drew his hand away and found blood upon his finger. Grace had the sudden, strange urge to reach out and press her handkerchief against it, and twisted her fingers together in front of her to resist actually acting on such preposterous thoughts. "What are you doing here?"

"What am I doing here?" she repeated, her eyes widening. Out of everything he could have said, she wouldn't have thought he would question anything regarding her actions. "I don't believe that is any of your concern, sir," she said, although she was well aware now that he was anything but gentlemanly. "I accompanied my father. I had no expectations of seeing you here, let alone in the middle of the boxing ring."

"I apologize for not living up to your expectations," he said, and she couldn't tell whether he was being honest or sarcastic. He was a hard man to read, and it seemed that he had reverted to his earlier character that had been present at the library — the man who she had these strange fantasies about, for no explainable reason.

"I-I have no expectations," she said. "I'm just not particularly… fond of violence, that is all."

"Yet you are here at a boxing match," he said, understandably confused.

"My father insisted," she said, before inhaling deeply and looking up at him. He was such a tall man, she had to crane her neck back to look him full in the face. "Did you really fix the match, as my father suggested?"

He dropped his gaze for a moment before returning it to her, his light green eyes glistening in an expression that she couldn't properly describe.

"Of course not," he said, but somehow, Grace knew that he was lying to her, and for reasons that were not at all rational, it hurt, deep within.

"Very well, then. I should go. My brother is waiting."

He nodded and then just as she was about to leave, he called out to her.

"Wait."

She paused, but never turned around to look at him.

"I don't even know your name," he said, his voice low, and she turned her head to the side, saying it just loud enough for him to hear.

"Grace."

CHAPTER 4

Grace.

It suited her.

He didn't even really know her, and yet he would guess that she likely lived up to her name in every way possible.

Damien was so deep within his thoughts that he forgot for a moment that Arie would be waiting for him. His brother stood within the doorway of the room where Damien took time to himself before and after fights. Damien shuttered his gaze as he entered, though Arie said nothing.

Arie glanced back at Ivan, who was waiting in the corner of the room with Damien's jacket. Damien finished doing up the top few buttons of his shirt before allowing Ivan to help him into his jacket, wincing as he shrugged his arms into the jacket's tight sleeves.

"We'll discuss this further at home," Arie said, and as Ivan patted his hands on Damien's shoulders in a gesture of support, Damien knew exactly what he was thinking — that he was glad that he wasn't in Damien's shoes.

"Very well," Damien said, already seeing his hot dinner and quick sleep ruined.

He said farewell to Ivan before he and Arie joined Xander and Juliet for the short ride home. They seemed to be well aware of the tension in the air and were silent for most of it until they arrived.

"Clean yourself up," Arie said to Damien as their sister, Diana, looked at them sharply, clearly well aware that something was amiss. Diana chose which fights to attend — she refused anytime she knew the match was fixed, asking what was the point of going when she already knew the outcome.

"I'll make sure your dinner is ready," she murmured, although her piercing stare, as perceptive as ever, cut through Damien as he walked away from her. He nodded a thanks as he trudged upstairs, heaving a sigh as he went.

Damien took his time bathing and dressing, but he couldn't put off the inevitable. He had only just sat down at the dining room table when Arie entered, taking the chair across from him. Damien wasn't fooled by his relaxed posture.

"Feeling better?" he asked, to which Damien grunted a response, not willing to take the time away from his pork and asparagus. Arie took great pride in the fact that he had stolen away a cook from one of the great houses of Mayfair.

"I'll take that as a yes," Arie said. "Now, I would ask you once more what happened in that fight, but it seems I have my answer."

Damien raised his eyebrows but said nothing in response.

"Mulberry's daughter," Arie said, and Damien nearly choked on the piece of chicken he had just bitten into. He coughed to clear his throat, somewhat surprised when Arie thumped him on the back to help. "I see I am correct. Have you slept with her?"

"No!" Damien forced out. "Of course not."

"Of course not? From what I know you've slept with half the women around here."

"I have not," Damien muttered.

"Say what you want, but I know far more than you think," Arie said as Diana took a seat beside him, sliding into the chair but saying nothing, though she was obviously intrigued. "What is the hold she has on you?"

"No hold," Damien grunted, his chewing slowing. He was beginning to lose his appetite the further this conversation went. "I hardly even know her. Have spoken to her once. Twice now."

"Then why did seeing her in the crowd cause you to lose focus? What could you possibly have had to say to her after the match?" Arie asked, his eyes glinting as he leaned over the table toward Damien. "You know we don't keep secrets from each other. Tell me what it is."

Damien lifted his head, taking a swallow of the ale Diana had placed in front of him before he answered Arie.

"The truth is, Arie, I don't keep secrets from you, but you keep plenty from us. Which is fine. I don't need to know all of the inner workings of your mind and, in fact, I don't believe I want to. But I've told you the truth. I don't know anything about her. I had met her earlier in the day and could tell she was surprised to see me in the ring. I just wanted to… explain myself."

Arie leaned back from the table, crossing his arms over his chest.

"I'm not entirely sure what you have to explain but you seem to be telling the truth."

Damien glowered at him. "Of course I am."

"Very well. What do you want with her, then?"

"Nothing."

"But you are interested."

"I never said that."

"You didn't have to." Arie tilted his head to the side, pausing for a moment as he studied Damien. "You know… as much as I still am not pleased about the match, perhaps this isn't as much of a problem as I originally thought. In fact, I believe it could prove quite useful."

"What is that supposed to mean?" Damien asked, instantly wary and no longer hungry. He hated when Arie got that look in his eyes. It meant that he had an idea, and one never knew the extent of Arie's ideas.

"I've been trying to learn more about Hugo Mulberry's business for some time now."

"He's in shipping, is he not?" Diana asked, adding her voice to the conversation for the first time.

"He is," Arie confirmed. "But there is more to his business than just shipping."

"Such as?" Diana asked, obviously more interested than Damien was, for Damien could see no positive ending to this conversation.

"He's also a smuggler," Arie said, his eyes glinting, and Damien frowned.

"A smuggler in London with a shipping operation? How has he not been caught?"

"He has another home in Dover and a son who lives there to run that end of the operations," Arie continued. "From there, he imports items from France and then brings them into London. He has a great many ships and his operation has grown. But he is able to keep it all hidden behind his legitimate business interests."

Damien stood now, unable to stay still any longer, the remains of his meal forgotten. He shook out his legs as he began to pace back and forth along the head of the table.

"What does any of this have to do with us?"

"We could *become* part of such an operation," Arie said, stretching his hands out to the side. "Perhaps not on the shipping end, but if we became the dealer for him here in London, we could make a sizeable sum, don't you think?"

Damien scratched his forehead, dislodging the piece of linen he had wrapped around one cut that refused to stop bleeding. "I don't know, Arie," he muttered, "seems a bit too convenient."

"Convenient is exactly right!" Arie exclaimed. "If you want to get close to Grace Mulberry, then you could learn more about her father's operations. Perhaps you could even get close enough that he might end up confiding some of his secrets in you. If he learns to trust you, then you could convince him to work with the family."

Damien stopped pacing to eye Arie with disbelief. "The man hates both of us. Just hours ago he was demanding our heads and our money. Grace told me that she abhors violence, right after she saw me beat Joe to the ground. There is no possible way that either of them are ever going to want anything to do with us."

He didn't add that while he would very much enjoy a reason to see Grace again, the thought of getting close to her for Arie's ulterior motives caused him more discomfort than he would like to admit. Which told him that he was already in far too deep, after knowing her for but one day. What the hell was wrong with him?

"Here's the thing, Damien," Arie said, standing himself before walking over to his brother. "You never know until you try."

* * *

"TELL ME MORE," Lydia demanded a few days later as she and Grace walked away from Grace's family home in Holborn. Grace was well aware that the house seemed like it belonged far more than their family did, but her father had insisted that they live in a neighborhood where they could remind the upper class that there was new money to be made, that one didn't need what he called a "fancy title" to have the house and the servants and all that came with it.

"There's not much to tell," Grace said with a shrug after she provided Lydia with all of the details of the night before. "I left after that."

"But he truly came after you?" Lydia asked, her eyes shining. "I suppose you're not the only one with an infatuation."

"I do *not* have an infatuation," Grace insisted. "Especially not after last night."

"I don't know," Lydia said with a shrug. "There is something incredibly masculine about a man who can speak with his fists."

"On that, we are in disagreement," Grace said, "for I think it is rather barbaric to beat another man with one's hands for no other reason than to entertain a crowd of people out for blood."

Lydia shrugged. "It's a tale as old as time. You know that."

She did, and yet she didn't have to like it.

"Are we still headed to the bookshop today?"

Grace bit her lip. She would like to say no, as she had no wish to encounter the fighter who stubbornly remained in her dreams again, but she had finished all of the books she had taken home with her last time and wouldn't mind a fresh stack. Besides, what were the chances he would be there again? It seemed every time she had been hoping to run into him in the past he had been absent, and even if she did catch sight of him, the reading room was big enough that she could hopefully avoid him.

"Yes," she said resolutely. "I won't let his possible presence keep me from enjoying the place that I love so much."

"That's the spirit," Lydia said, always one to face any potential adversity head-on. Lydia's father was a furniture manufacturer and his sense of risk had been passed down to his only daughter, who longed to run the family business one day, despite knowing there was no chance of such an occurrence. "Besides, if you're still attracted to him, what's keeping you from a flirtation? It doesn't mean that you have to marry the man."

Grace looked at her with eyes so wide that Lydia started laughing, causing a few passersby to turn their way.

"Oh, don't look at me like that. It's about time that you enjoyed what a good man has to offer. I've hardly ever seen you look twice at a man before, so you can understand why I'm rather excited about your enthusiasm over this one."

"It was just a stupid imagining, Lydia," Grace muttered, having no wish to speak of it further. "Don't think on it anymore."

"If you say so," Lydia said, although her dancing blue eyes told Grace an entirely different story.

Grace pushed open the door of the bookshop with great trepidation. She had tried to make Lydia enter first, but Lydia, of course, had insisted that Grace go ahead of her. Grace looked around furiously when she stepped through the door, but let out a great sigh of relief when she found no sight of the hulking brute she had watched in the ring last night. She smiled warmly at the man behind the counter, and the clerk took her books with an answering smile.

"Hello, Mr. Moon," she said, and he nodded back at her in greeting.

"We actually have a question for you."

Grace started at Lydia's nearness, then turned around and tried to signal with her eyes that she had no wish to ask anything further of the clerk at the moment. She was just about to step down from the platform that housed his desk when Lydia continued. "There is a man that comes in here now and then. To read. Much taller, broader than any other patron you likely receive. What is it that he likes to read, Grace?"

Grace shot her friend a furious look, but she couldn't help answering her anyway. "Adventure."

"Adventure," Lydia confirmed. "Fiction, I am sure."

"Oh, him!" Mr. Moon said after a moment as he nodded before pushing his glasses up his nose. "Yes, I do know who you mean. I haven't seen him in a few days but he usually comes in once or twice a week if that helps you at all. Around this time, actually." He scratched his forehead for a moment as though suddenly wondering just why they were asking such questions. "Is there anything else I can help you with? Anything about a book that you might be interested in?"

"Nothing else, but you have been very helpful, Mr. Moon." Lydia beamed at the clerk, who had obviously always been quite taken with her, before pulling Grace deeper into the bookshop, through the door and into the reading room.

"There we are. Now all we have to do is wait."

"Wait?" Grace placed her hands on her hips. "You mean find our books as quickly as we can and take our leave?"

Lydia sighed. "You are no fun. But very well, if that's what you want."

"That is what I want."

Grace was still looking at Lydia when she turned to make her way to the shelves which housed the romance novels she loved so much.

And walked right into a wall.

CHAPTER 5

Damien had been so busy surveying the outskirts of the reading room for Grace that he hadn't been looking in front of him.

Until she walked right into his chest.

He reached down to steady her, his large hands wrapping around her wrists, reminding him of how different they were in so many ways.

An unexpected thrill ran through him at seeing her again, even as he cursed himself for being so happy about it. He had no right to search her out. In fact, he should be doing everything he could to resist this scheme of Arie's.

But his brother had continued to remind him to trust him, that everything had always worked out before, so why wouldn't it now? He had also promised Damien that he had no wish to do anything that would violate Grace's trust, that he wanted only to work *with* her father, not against him.

Damien supposed he would have to believe him. He *had* believed in him for nearly thirty years now, and he didn't need Arie to remind him that without him, he would be nothing, that Arie had provided him with everything he could ever ask for and that he needed to trust him to continue moving forward.

Their siblings, Calli and Xander, had both had reason to question Arie's motives as of late, but all had worked out for them, had it not? Damien just needed to trust in his family and that everything would be fine. What else could he do?

But when he looked down at the woman he now held in his arms, he nearly forgot about everything Arie had said.

"Miss Mulberry," he murmured. "Lovely to see you again."

"I wish I could say the same," she said, and he lifted his brows at the spark in her voice. "I wasn't sure that I would see you again after the other night."

"That you would see me again, or that you would want to?" he asked, unable to resist teasing her as one side of his lips tilted upward in a smile.

She was saved from answering him by her friend, who stepped up nearly between them and beamed up at him.

"You must be Damien Hondros. I am Lydia Campbell."

"A pleasure to meet you," he murmured, bowing to her as though she was part of the *ton,* and she blushed. When he glanced over at Grace, he was pleased to see that she didn't seem entirely happy to watch the exchange. Perhaps she was more interested in him than she let on.

"We were just leaving," Grace said as began toward the door, walking by the clerk's desk. Damien kept pace with her.

A throat cleared behind him.

"Oh, yes, forgive me. May I introduce my sister, Miss Diana Hondros? Diana, this is Miss Mulberry and Miss Campbell."

"Lovely to meet you," Diana said, although her pointed stare made her curiosity far too obvious. Damien had to refrain from rolling his eyes. Diana had insisted on accompanying him, telling him that she needed to understand what "all the fuss" was about.

"I didn't think you would be here today," Grace said, drawing back her shoulders in a gesture that made it all too aware that she actually had no *wish* to see him today. She had only come here because of that supposition.

"I am a man of many interests, Miss Mulberry," he said with a nod even as his cheeks warmed slightly, much to his chagrin.

"So it would seem."

Damien felt a finger dig into his side, and he had to work to keep his expression from revealing his annoyance at Diana, although she did remind him of why he was here — to try to get closer to Grace.

He held out his arm when they pushed through the door. "The weather is pleasant today. Would you care to walk? I should like to speak to you about a couple of things."

Grace looked up at him warily, but then Damien noticed her friend nudge her in the back.

"Very well," she said with a sigh as well and a look behind her at Miss Campbell — a look that caused Damien to smile as he could only guess how much chagrin it contained.

Grace placed her fingers on his arm as he began to lead her down Piccadilly Street, Diana and Miss Campbell falling in behind them. Damien could only imagine what kind of conversation they might strike up, but at the moment he would have to simply trust that Diana would keep Miss Campbell entertained enough to not care about his own discussion.

He cleared his throat as he tried to decide where to begin. He wished he had Xander's gift of knowing what to say in nearly every exchange, of holding the charm and appeal that made every woman fall at his feet.

But, alas, Damien would have to make do with what he

had — namely, the ability to be honest and, hopefully, come across as trustworthy as he always tried to be.

"I wanted you to know that what you saw the other night… that's not exactly who I am," he said, scratching his forehead with his other hand.

"You said as much after your match," Grace said, her gaze forward. "But the truth is, Mr. Hondros—"

"Damien, please."

"The truth is, Damien, that it doesn't overly matter what I think. If that is how you wish to make your living, then so be it. You don't have to pretend to be someone you are not in order to impress me. In fact, I'm not entirely sure just why you feel you have to be a certain man with me at all."

Damien didn't know either, but he didn't know how to tell her that. Or why, for the first time in his life, he wanted someone to understand who he truly was and not just who he presented to the world. He had never worried before what a young woman might think. In fact, most women that he knew fell at his feet with praise for him and wanted to watch his matches even more, for that was what had attracted them to him in the first place.

Not this one, it seemed.

"Perhaps it's because I want to get to know you better," he said straightforwardly. "And I don't like the thought of you thinking less of me."

Grace stopped then, and he had to urge her forward so that Diana and Miss Campbell wouldn't completely catch up and join their conversation. Damien wanted more time alone with her first.

"You—you want to get to know *me*?"

"Well, yes," he said with a bit of laughter. "Who else might I be talking about, Miss Campbell?"

"You did seem quite pleased to meet her," she mumbled so

lowly as she looked off to the side that he nearly didn't hear her.

Damien couldn't help but laugh at that. "So you *were* jealous. I thought as much."

"Jealous?" she finally turned to look at him, her mouth agape. "Of course I'm not *jealous*. I have no reason to be jealous. I—"

Her astonishment finally turned into a small smile, however, when she must have caught his teasing glance. "You are jesting with me."

"I am."

"You don't seem like the type of man who jests often."

"I'm usually not," he acknowledged with a dip of his head. "Perhaps you bring out a different side of me, Miss Mulberry."

"Grace is fine."

"I'm glad to hear it, as that is how I already think of you."

"You do?" Her warm brown eyes looked up at him with some question. "That is hardly proper of you."

"As you have seen, I am not exactly the most proper of men," he said, unable to help the chagrin that accompanied the words. "Which brings me to the point that I do understand if you don't feel that it is in your best interests to see me again."

"I wasn't aware that we had any plans to see one another again."

"We don't—yet."

She looked down at their feet for a moment as though she was somewhat embarrassed, only bringing her gaze up when he suddenly pulled her toward him in order to move her from the path of a passing cart.

"Thank you," she murmured before breathing deeply as though trying to fill herself with courage. "What I don't quite understand, Mr. Ho — Damien — is why me? I realize I am not exactly the type of woman to evoke much passion. I most certainly have never had men falling at my feet or pounding on my father's door."

While she didn't entirely turn to look at him, when he leaned down to peek past her bonnet, he could see that her cheeks were a flaming pink. He found it rather endearing.

"Then I believe that most men haven't had the opportunity to see the woman you really are."

"You have no idea who I am."

"That is true. But I would like to try to find out."

"Who do you *think* I am, Damien?"

Damien took that as a sign that she might be loosening her reserve against him and continued a bit more confidently.

"Well, you are obviously a woman with great imagination."

"Why would you think that?" she asked, obviously startled.

"Because of how much you read, of course," he said. "I saw you just returned four books — four books that you only borrowed a few days ago. A woman who reads as much fiction as you would likely have many stories of her own running around her head."

She didn't say anything, which led him to believe that he was correct, and he continued.

"You have great love for your family."

"Do you know much of my family?"

"I know who your father is, of course. I know he is quite successful and has built himself up from the same neighborhoods that my brother did. It must take a man of great determination to do so. The fact that you would accompany him to a boxing match that you had no wish to attend says much about your responsibility and dedication as a daughter. I also think you are a woman of great independence."

"Oh?"

"Your brother allowed you to stay behind and talk to me. You visit the bookshop alone but for a friend. Your family allows you freedoms that not many women are afforded."

"They do," she said, a small smile teasing her lips. Part of it was because they were all too busy to take the time to watch over her, but she wasn't about to complain. "I am lucky."

"And you are a woman of great beauty."

She chuckled at that. "You are a flatterer, Damien, but you are now also a liar."

"Never," he said vehemently, wondering why she would think so. She may not have been a classic beauty like others, but her heart-shaped face with voluminous eyes and pert lips called to him. When she spoke of something she was passionate about, her entire body became animated and drew him in. Then there were those curves… "You have beauty within you and around you, Grace, and I would like to draw more of it out of you."

"You can do so, can you?" she asked, turning to him with a raised eyebrow. "That is quite the skill, Damien. Perhaps you should add magician to your many talents."

"Perhaps I should. But I don't need to. Not with you."

"You seem to have gathered a great deal of impressions about me, Damien — most of them, actually, surprisingly accurate — but the truth is, I still have no idea what to think of you. You seem to be two different men, and those are only two of the sides I have seen of you in a short time. Are there more that I am missing?"

"No," he said, shaking his head. "This is me. The man in front of you today, I promise you that. But I can understand why you might be suspicious."

He looked behind them, seeing that Diana and Miss Campbell had dropped behind a bit. He realized he was likely walking far faster than any of the women could easily match, although Grace seemed to have kept up with him. He wondered if she was used to doing so, growing up with as many brothers as she had.

He stopped, turning to her and obviously surprising her when he took both of her hands in his.

"I will ask you this, Grace," he said, more softly now, looking down at her imploringly. He hadn't realized how much shorter she was than he, her presence obviously seeming much larger than her own height. "Provide us the chance to get to know one another better. Let me see you again. If you learn more about me and decide that I am not a man you'd like to know better, I'll understand. But let me try to show you who I really am, to convince you that the Damien before you is the Damien I am at heart."

She seemed torn, but didn't pull her hands away.

"What are you suggesting?"

"My family is hosting a masquerade at the gaming hell my brother owns — the same one where the boxing match was held."

"Of course your brother owns a gaming hell."

Damien considered that her own father was a smuggler, but didn't think it was prudent to mention such a thing at the moment.

"He does," he said instead. "The guests attending the masquerade will be from all walks of life, but it is always enjoyable, and, I promise, there will be no risk to you once you are within the doors. We will ensure your safety — I promise you that."

"I don't know," she said, looking to the side as though hoping Miss Campbell would appear and make the decision for her. "I'm not sure if it's something that I should attend."

"You don't have to decide in this moment," Damien said, not wanting to pressure her as much as he desperately hoped she would agree. He released one of her hands to reach into an inside pocket of his jacket, pulling out a small card. "Here is the information and address, although I'm sure you already know where to find it. Bring one of your brothers if you would like. Hell, bring all of them. But I would love to see you there."

"We shall see," she murmured, and Damien had to accept that it was better than a no. Diana and Miss Campbell had finally caught up to them, and Grace looked around as though only now realizing where they were.

"This is close to my home," she said. "Miss Campbell and I best go. Thank you for the walk, Mr. Hondros. Miss Hondros, it was a pleasure to meet you."

"Goodbye, Miss Mulberry," Damien murmured as Diana came to stop beside him, looking up at him with interest.

"Is all well, brother?"

"I hope so, Diana. I really do."

CHAPTER 6

"This was a terrible idea."

"How can you say that?" Lydia looked at Grace indignantly as they stood on the bottom step, staring up at the imposing red brick structure before them whose walls seemed to be straining. "It looks like great fun. And you look extraordinary. Damien Hondros is not going to take his eyes off you."

"That's what I'm afraid of," Grace murmured as she readjusted the satin mask covering her face for what seemed like the countless time. The aquamarine mask with gold sequins matched her dress, which gave her the look of a mermaid — an ode to her father's shipping company, although whether anyone here would recognize it as such, she had no idea.

Borden was already up the stairs, holding the door open for the two women. He had been as ecstatic as Lydia at having been invited to the event that he told Grace was nearly impossible to ever achieve an invitation for, although Jeremiah was quick to point out that he already had a way in. Borden wasn't entirely pleased to hear that, and also was sure to inform Grace that he had no idea how she had pulled off her own invitation. Once he had learned about it, there was no way that Grace could ever say no. It obviously meant far too much to her best friend and her brother.

Grace, however, was much more concerned now than she had previously been as she looked at all of the people around her — those entering beside them and those who had already gathered in the foyer. Damien hadn't been lying when he said that all walks of life would be invited. There was every type of person here, from men and women who seemed as elegant as lords and ladies to women so scantily clad that they could only be working for one of the establishments nearby — or perhaps this very one.

Grace was suddenly rather overcome by the reminder of the world Damien inhabited, her mind beginning to wander as she wondered about his involvement with the women who likely worked for his family.

"Enough," she chastised herself, reminding herself that she had no reason to care.

"What was that?" Lydia asked, but Grace waved away her question.

"Let's get this over with, shall we?"

Lydia and Borden shared a look of amusement at Grace's attitude toward the entire event, but it was difficult to say much more when they were quickly engulfed by the sudden chaos of the room.

It was a symphony of music, light, color, and perfumes. Of people, everywhere. Grace guessed that the large, two-tiered room was typically full of tables, but tonight it was open for guests to mill about. Some were dancing, others were drinking, and still more were openly flirting, some men and women in such suggestive embraces and positions that Grace gasped aloud.

"Best we don't tell Father exactly what this event included, all right?" Borden said in her ear, to which Grace could only nod, so overcome was she by all that assaulted her senses.

Musicians in the corner played a jaunty tune, barmaids yelled out orders, while men called out to the women – and each other – from across the room. There was a lemony scent to the air, as though someone had recently cleaned the room, but it was quickly being replaced by the odours of many bodies close together and the alcohol that was filling them.

A large chandelier hung from the ceiling in the middle of the room, while long, heavy crimson curtains covered the windows, and landscapes and portraits of white marble buildings and the sea decorated the walls. It was actually much more refined than Grace would ever have imagined.

She knew her father had some background of disrepute, but never in her life had she attended such a thing. She might not be a lady, but she had been raised with some of the same sensibilities as one. Her mother had made sure of that. "You two stay in the main room, all right?" Borden said, even as his head was already swivelling around as though he could hardly take it all in. "I won't be far if you need me."

Grace and Lydia shared a look, but Lydia nodded, enthusiastically agreeing, which only worried Grace as her friend always had ideas that often ended badly.

"Of course. We shall be on our best behaviour, won't we Grace?"

"Of course," Grace agreed, although Lydia's best behaviour was, at times, rather suspect. Lydia herself looked quite the siren tonight, dressed in a deep crimson silk gown with black piping and a matching mask. Her red hair was curled around her shoulders, and Grace hadn't missed even Borden's approving perusal of her.

As soon as Borden left, Lydia turned to Grace, her eyes shining.

"What shall we do first?" she asked, to which Grace could only answer, "Do?"

Before Lydia could continue with whatever ideas were wandering inside her head, however, she was approached by a tall gentleman who seemed, at least on the surface, to be rather polite.

"Forgive me for my boldness, but you could not help but catch my eye the moment you entered the room," the man said, reaching for Lydia's hand and then bringing it to his lips. "Would you dance with me?"

The dance was nothing like what Grace had always imagined a proper ball to be, but that did not seem to bother Lydia in the slightest. "I would love to," she said, before pausing as she obviously remembered Grace, "only my friend—"

"Will also be dancing. With me."

Grace whirled around at the gravelly voice that sounded in her ear, finding a masked man standing behind her — a man who could never be disguised.

"Damien," she said stupidly, as she recognized Lydia being led away.

"You came," he said, his lips curling into a smile — lips that she hadn't paid much attention to before, not until now when they were showcased beneath the plain black mask which covered his eyes.

"I did," she said. "Lydia insisted."

Realizing with some horror that she was basically telling him that she had no wish to be there, she quickly added, "not that I didn't want to come. I was just—unsure. My brother also accompanied us."

"Which one?"

"Borden."

"He was with you at the fight?"

"He was."

They stood there awkwardly for a moment as Grace searched for something to say, but Damien saved her when he reached out a hand.

"Shall we?"

"Shall we…"

"Dance, of course," he said, his eyes crinkling as his lips lifted into a smile, and Grace was grateful that the mask hid some of the reddening of her face.

"I suppose," she said, even though she was not particularly enthralled by the idea. "I must warn you however… I am not sure if I much live up to my namesake."

"No?" He raised an eyebrow.

"I will try valiantly, however," she said, lifting her chin. "That will never be an issue."

"That is all one can ask," Damien said, nodding his head toward her as they weaved between people toward the dance floor, Grace's hand clasped within Damien's. Even through their gloves, she could feel the heat radiating off him, a heat that she suddenly had this strange wish to wrap herself in, as ridiculous as the idea was.

Grace could feel eyes upon her, and she wasn't sure if it was because she was accompanying Damien or if it was because most people here would have no idea as to her identity. Suddenly she was extremely grateful that the event was a masquerade.

"You look beautiful tonight," Damien said as he took one of her hands in his and placed the other on her waist while they began something akin to a waltz, although a dance much livelier and not nearly as proper nor as choreographed.

"Thank you," she said. "I wasn't sure what to wear, but from what I have seen thus far, there would be no wrong answer."

"No, anything goes here at Arie's establishment," Damien said as he led her through the steps in surprising elegance for his size. She supposed that much of his finesse was transferred from the boxing ring. While she may not have been a fan of the violence, she could, at least, appreciate the athleticism required for such a sport.

Grace tried to concentrate on his words and not the hand that was wrapped around hers, nor the touch of his other hand on her waist.

"He is your brother, then — Arie Hondros?"

"In nearly every way," Damien said with a nod. "Every way except blood."

"Oh," Grace said with some surprise. "I had no idea."

"Out of my entire family, Calli and Xander are the only two who are blood related," he explained. "The rest of us were brought together because we needed a home. Arie has a way of understanding just when someone needs help. He may not always seem the most generous or considerate, but he has a side to him that looks after those he cares for — in his own way."

"I see," Grace said, suddenly overcome by her interest in learning more about Damien and the Hondros family, but unsure of how to ask more without being overtly curious.

"It's all right," Damien said gently as though he could read her mind. "Ask away."

"Very well," Grace said cautiously. "How old were you when you joined Arie's… family?"

"I was actually his first sibling," Damien said, his eyes taking on a faraway look as he was obviously transported back to the past, to whenever this had occurred. "I was but a babe, born to a courtesan who died shortly after my birth while on the ship here to England. I don't know where I would have ended up if Arie hadn't found me and taken me in."

"Where were you coming from?" Grace asked, unable to stop her inquisition.

"Greece."

"How old was Arie?"

"Twelve."

"Twelve? And he was suddenly responsible for a baby?" she asked, aghast.

"He had help from some of the women who created a community of sorts upon their arrival — at least at first. But from the time I turned two, we were on our own."

"My goodness," Grace murmured, unable to hide her shock. She would never have imagined such behaviour from a man like Arie Hondros, but then, she didn't actually know anything about him. Her first impressions of this family were proving more and more inaccurate. "And your siblings?"

"We took in Diana soon afterward. She was nearly five and would have been sent to a workhouse, where she likely wouldn't have lasted very long. Most children don't. Calli and Xander came as a pair shortly after that. They were together and likely would have made it through, but they were a good… fit for our family."

"Arie has created much success for himself."

"He has," Damien said, although it seemed obvious that he didn't have any more to say on the subject.

"Do you all still live together?"

"We live in this neighbourhood," Damien said, meeting her eyes once more. "Calli and Xander have both married, although Xander and his wife are not far."

"And Calli?"

That question elicited a true grin from Xander.

"She lives in Mayfair. Married to the Duke of Hargreaves."

Grace gasped before immediately lifting her hand from Damien's shoulder to cover her mouth. "My apologies, I am just—"

"Shocked? So were we. But it has all worked out quite well."

The song came to an end, and Damien bowed to her as though they were at a fancy ball. "Would you like to dance again, Grace? I promise that here, there will be no judgements and you will not be required to marry me."

His eyes twinkled and Grace was aghast at how those words caused such a tingle to course through her.

"Of course not," she said. "I—"

She looked around, seeing that curiosity was growing, and despite Damien's words, she knew that the longer she stayed at his side, the more attention she would receive. Lydia seemed quite content to continue dancing with her admirer and Borden was nowhere to be found.

"Perhaps we could find somewhere a bit… quieter?"

"Of course," Damien said, offering her his arm. "I know of just the place."

He led her back around the room, twisting and turning in a dance all of its own, as he took her deeper within the building until they came to a set of stairs.

"Ladies first," he said, and then must have caught her look of unease. "I promise I will do nothing that you might find… untoward."

For some reason, even though she knew she was likely being a fool, Grace trusted him. Besides, they were still within shouting distance of the main room if anything happened. Whether anyone would care, well, that was another issue entirely.

She lifted her skirts as she and Damien twisted around the winding staircase, until they came to a room — one with a railing all along the front of it.

Damien led her to the balcony, stretching his hand out in front of them.

"From here, you can see anything and everything you'd

like — while most people have no thought to ever look above them," he said with a smile. "And if you stand back far enough, they cannot see you at all."

"Goodness," Grace murmured, picking out Lydia and finally Borden. "This is what you use to watch gamblers, is it?"

"It is," he confirmed. "It is where I am stationed most nights, to observe and determine if my… attention is needed."

"And then what do you do?"

"Deal with it," he said, obviously uncomfortable at the question.

"With your fists?" she couldn't help but ask, to which he nodded. He didn't seem much capable of telling a lie, and she appreciated that, if nothing else, he didn't hide the truth from her. "Do you enjoy this type of work?" she asked, unable to help herself.

"No," he said shortly, "but it's what I'm good at."

She nodded, sad that he would have to spend such time doing something he obviously hated. But then, how many people had to do the same, in one way or another?

"Would you care to dance again?" he asked, stepping back and holding a hand out toward her. "This time, no one will be watching, so there is nothing for you to worry about."

"How did you know that I cared about that?" she asked, curious as she thought she had hidden it rather well.

"The tension in your back. The concern in your eyes. The tightness of your jaw."

"Is there anything that you *don't* see?" she asked, mesmerized now by the intensity of his own expression.

"Nothing."

This time when he took her in his arms, he whirled her around in an expression of great artistry, and her slight squeal slipped out unbidden. She felt weightless in his arms, which she never would have thought possible.

Everything about him told her that he was entirely wrong for her, but being held in his arms like this? Nothing had ever felt so right.

CHAPTER 7

Damien had always secretly enjoyed the dance lessons that Arie had forced them to complete. His siblings had complained tirelessly about them, groaning on and on that they would never use such skills.

They had all been wrong — it seemed that Arie was almost always right, as he was sure to remind them — but Damien had never been more grateful for learning those steps than in this moment.

He didn't have much to offer a woman like Grace Mulberry. She might not be of the bluest blood herself, but she carried herself with a certain class, an intelligence and maturity that was far beyond most of the women he associated with.

He also knew that she had no reason to want to spend more time with a man like him.

But she was here. And he was going to make the most of it.

Arie would be livid to find out that he had brought her up here, an area reserved for family and employees of the gaming hell. Arie prided himself on his establishment, one that ran nearly without effort as he far preferred his work of another sort — work that sometimes crossed over to his ownership here.

Instead, Arie entrusted Damien with much of the responsibility of the club, and it had become a place where Damien spent much of his time. So Damien decided that it was up to him just how he would spend it tonight. He was supposed to be keeping watch over the party, to escort out any undesirables. Who said he had to do it alone?

Damien wished he could see the entirety of Grace's face as he turned her around, in a waltz that he flavored with his own style. He couldn't help that her every movement, every touch affected him in ways that another woman's never would.

Her swirling skirts brushed against his thighs, her hand warmed in his, her fingers ran up and down his shoulder so lightly that he wondered whether she even realized what she was doing.

Her brown eyes caught his, and in them he could see the same astonishment that he felt — wondering at what was flowing between them, at how they had entered into some unspoken understanding, the realization that perhaps there was more to him than she had imagined when she saw him in the boxing ring.

At least, he hoped she was thinking such a thing.

When the music from below finally ebbed, he took their clasped hands and twirled her once, slowly, until she came to a halt in front of him, her skirts the last thing to settle as they stood there, but a hair's breadth away from one another.

He leaned down, his breath catching as her plump pink lips appeared before his. She was a full head shorter than he, and he knew he would have to dip his head to catch them. The question was… should he?

"You were wrong," he said in a low voice, and her lashes flew up as her eyes rose to meet his.

"About what?" she said, her voice breathy, and Damien had to resist a smug smile that she was as affected as he.

"You do live up to your name. Your dancing is admirable."

"You are an excellent leader."

"It's easy with the right partner."

Pink flooded into her cheeks once more, but Damien wouldn't have that. He reached down, placing his index finger beneath her chin then tipped it up so that she was looking at him again.

"On that, you are correct. We fit well together."

She stood still for a moment as though in shock, and Damien was ready for her to push him away, to which he would step back regretfully but understandingly.

After her momentary hesitation she lifted her hands and Damien began to pull away, anticipating them shoving into his chest.

But it was his turn to be surprised. For she reached up and gripped the lapels of his jacket, pulling him back down toward her as though to say she had no intention for him to go anywhere.

To which he eagerly agreed.

Damien wrapped his arms around her back, pulling her snug against him. She let out a slight squeal, although it would go unheard to anyone but him, for he drank in every sound she made. As her thighs pressed against his and his hip fit into the curve of her waist, he teased her lips with his tongue until she opened to him, and he swept it inside, exploring the velvet of her mouth as he lost himself in her inviting curves around him.

He could spend all night in here with her, and he nearly lost his head and proceeded — which he knew they would both regret, for she was not a woman to give herself to a man in such a circumstance. Or, perhaps, any circumstance but the one to be expected of her.

Despite all of that tugging on the back of his mind, it was not Damien who first roused himself from the spell that had been cast around them, one of their own doing, whether or not they had realized it. No, it was Grace who first lifted her head, her rosy, bruised lips forming words that he didn't at first hear, so caught up was he in the perfection surrounding him.

"Did you hear that?" she must have repeated, as she shook his shoulders this time, and he finally came out of his stupor.

"Hear what?"

"Those sounds. It almost seems as if—"

The crash resounded below him, and Damien left Grace from where he had been kissing her against the wall, running over to the edge of the balcony and peering down before him.

A small circle had formed in the middle of the crowd around two men — opponents, it seemed — as they stepped back and forth, throwing punches that were sometimes ducked beneath and other times found purchase.

"Oh, shit," Damien said, wiping a hand across a forehead. "I've got to go," he said, not having time to look back behind him at Grace as he ran down the stairs. "Stay here and whatever you do, do *not* go to the railing."

He only prayed that she would listen to his instructions as he ran into the fracas.

* * *

GRACE HELD one hand over her tingling lips, the other over her heart as though she could slow its frantic beating. Had Damien really just kissed her? And not just kissed her... but taken over her body and soul in a nearly indescribable way?

It was everything she had ever dreamed of, since the moment she had first seen him in the bookshop.

She closed her eyes, recalling the day she had walked into the reading room and seen his large frame bent over the book, which seemed tiny in his meaty hands.

Hands that she had imagined running over her — hands that had held her today.

She drew a shaky breath to settle herself, but the shout from below brought her back to reality faster than anything else possibly could. She remembered Damien's warning to stay away from the railing, but from what she could tell of the angles of the balcony, as long as she stayed a few steps back from the edge, no one below could see her.

Grace had just made it far enough that she could see what was happening below her, when Damien rushed into the small circle where two men were obviously either fighting or preparing to. Without any sign of fear or hesitation, he stood in the middle of them, holding one hand out to each of them as he was obviously trying to broker peace.

His attempts, however, were clearly not met with much acceptance as the shorter but drunker man, his shirt now torn with a trickle of blood running down the front, attempted to run through Damien to get to the man who had apparently wronged him.

It didn't end well for him.

Damien held an arm out, and the man ran right into it, his head snapping back, the rest of his body following suit. He still managed to try to get up, but before he could gather his feet below him, Damien must have received an order from someone else for his attention was caught for just a second before he looked down, pulled back his arm, and punched the man in the face.

Grace gasped aloud, clapping her hand over her mouth as she ran a few steps backward, hiding the scene from her vision. She couldn't keep herself from watching, however, and before she even knew what she was doing, she had crept forward just far enough that she could see what was below her again.

The man disappeared from her sight, likely falling to the floor for a moment before Damien reached down, picked him up, and slung him over his shoulders as though he weighed no more than a small woman.

Perhaps that was why he had been able to pick her up and twirl her with ease. He was even stronger than he appeared — which was saying something.

Grace didn't think she could ever forget how he had looked shirtless in the boxing ring. His muscles were perfectly sculpted, marred only by the small scars and nicks that covered them — not a man who had ever met with any great peril, but who had obviously spent a life in scrapes.

She had been too horrified during the match to notice, but she had certainly remembered. Every time she did her mouth had nearly dried completely.

Now was similar. For all that she had just witnessed seemed to erase the entirety of what had just happened between them. Grace squeezed her eyes shut, trying to remember the man who had danced with her, below and up here, the man who had walked with her like a gentleman, who'd treated her like a person with intelligent thoughts and opinions.

But all of that was lost to the violence in front of her, the man who seemed to have no issue with using his strength in ways that only hurt others.

Grace went from motionless to a sprint in seconds. She looked wildly around for the stairs before running to them, nearly tripping over the top few steps in her haste as she grabbed on to the banister, half-racing, half-falling down the rest of the stairs. Fortunately, she immediately saw Lydia's black-and-red costume, and she ran over to her, grabbing onto her arm before tugging her away from the crush of people.

"Lydia, we have to go."

"But—"

"Please!" Grace turned her face imploringly to her friend, who seemed to read the urgency in it.

"Very well," Lydia said with a look of regret at the man from whose embrace Grace's insistence had forced her to step away from. "But first we have to find Borden."

"Borden could be anywhere," Grace said, as she tried to ignore the scene beside her, though it was rather hard to miss. Damien was carrying out the man he had sent to the floor and then picked up. Before he walked out, he pointed at the other man, saying something that Grace couldn't hear but she could only assume was a threat.

She tugged at Lydia's arm, desperate to leave before Damien returned.

"Let's go. *Now*. We'll take the carriage so that Borden will know we've left with it."

Lydia reluctantly nodded her agreement.

"Very well. But as soon as we leave, you *must* tell me what's caused such urgency."

With Lydia, Grace knew that she had no choice but to agree.

CHAPTER 8

Damien took a deep breath as he stood on the top step of the third townhouse from the corner on Bedford Road in front of the large brass doorknocker that seemed to be eyeing him warily.

He had done many different things in his life — most of them questionable — but he had never done this.

Knocked on the door of a woman he was interested in — for reasons other than carnal.

Arie, however, had insisted. He had, most unfortunately, witnessed Grace fleeing their establishment last evening — right after Damien had left her.

When he had returned from dealing with the men who had tried to turn the masquerade into their own personal boxing match, he had hurried upstairs back to Grace, praying that she had listened to him and remained.

Only to find that she had disappeared.

It wasn't until Damien returned downstairs that Arie told him he had seen Grace and her friend exiting the building shortly after Damien had left with one of the unruly characters in tow.

"Why would she leave?" he had asked Diana later, unsure just what the next step forward was. Diana had looked at him as though he had no sense at all before rolling her eyes and asking him just what had prevented Grace from placing her trust in him in the first place.

He realized then just what Diana was getting at — if Grace hated the violence of the boxing ring, what must she have thought of him had she been watching how he had dealt with the exchange at the masquerade?

He tried to see it from her perspective. For him, it had been a part of his life for so long that he hardly thought anything of it. He had a skill, one that they put into use when necessary.

It would be much different for Grace.

Diana had told him that there was only one thing to do — apologize and explain. Arie had agreed that it was the best idea. Damien had reluctantly followed through, as hesitant as he had been to do so — but first, he'd made a couple of stops.

Now here he was, at a house full of men who likely lived to protect their little sister.

He gave his shoulders a little shake before knocking on the door.

Damien wasn't sure what he had expected at the household of a merchant like Mulberry, but the man must be doing fairly well for himself, for a butler opened the door, albeit a rather young one.

"Good day," the man said. "May I help you? I'm afraid that Mr. Mulberry is not in at the moment."

"That's fine," Damien said, the cowardly part of him hoping that Grace would also be out and he could leave this for another day, while the somewhat braver side of him was still looking forward to seeing her, despite the misgivings she likely held toward him. "I'm actually here to see Miss Mulberry."

"Miss Mulberry?" The butler's eyebrows rose in interest. "I will see if she is receiving visitors. You may come in."

Damien stood awkwardly in the foyer, shifting his weight from one foot to the other as he waited for the butler to return. The house was rather lavishly decorated, with furniture, paintings, floral arrangements, and decorative dishes practically sitting on top of one another. It didn't take him long to determine just who was behind the design.

"Oh, good afternoon! Come in, come in, sir. We were not expecting any visitors, but we are always happy to host one of Grace's gentleman callers, are we not?"

A woman who looked a great deal like Grace but with perhaps less… grace appeared in the drawing room beyond the entrance, her arms outstretched toward Damien. He had no idea whether he was supposed to walk into her embrace, remain where he was, or follow her into the room.

Fortunately, Grace appeared beside the woman, who must be her mother, saving him from making the wrong decision.

"Mr. Hondros," she said, her words formal and stiff, although her eyes belied her indifference. "What brings you here today?"

"Grace," her mother hissed in her ear, "can we not welcome the poor man into the drawing room?"

Grace turned a look of disbelief upon her mother, but the woman was obviously not one who was ever deterred, for she pushed past her daughter's resistance and joined Damien across the room, taking his hand in hers.

"Come, come, have a seat," she said, a welcoming smile crossing her wide cheeks. "Unfortunately, my husband and my sons are out on business at the moment, but Grace and I are here to entertain. Maria! Tea please! Sit right here," she pointed to the corner of a small settee, "and Grace, you will join him on the other side."

"Mother—"

"I shall sit here," she took a chair across from them, "and you shall tell me how the two of you know one another."

When Grace dutifully sat, Damien received the impression that Mrs. Mulberry was the type of woman who most people found it was easier to simply acquiesce with her than to argue — it had always been similar with Diana.

Of course, her mother's efforts didn't stop Grace from bestowing upon him a glare that told him exactly what she thought of him showing up here at her home, unannounced. Damien channeled his brother Xander's charm and grinned at her instead — which wasn't particularly difficult, for the truth was, he rather liked Mrs. Mulberry and her enthusiasm, although he could see why it might be rather trying to be one of her children.

"We met at the bookshop," Damien said when Mrs. Mulberry stared at them both, waiting for an answer.

"The bookshop?" she said, her eyes rounding. "How interesting. Do you visit there often?"

"Yes, I do, actually," Damien said, and Mrs. Mulberry turned her excited expression to her daughter, smiling encouragingly.

"Did you hear that, Grace? A man who enjoys reading enough to visit the bookshop. Why, I cannot imagine your father or your brothers ever doing such a thing!"

"Nor can I, Mother."

"And that is where the two of you met?"

"We did," Damien said with a nod. "Although I should say that it was actually *outside* of the bookshop, when a horse was spooked and almost hit Grace. Fortunately, I was in the right place at the right moment and was able to protect her."

Mrs. Mulberry was now sitting so far forward on the seat of her chair that Damien was afraid she was going to fall off into the tea tray that the maid had just delivered. He wasn't sure that he could properly extricate her from such an event.

He was so focused on the woman's precarious situation that he had forgotten to watch Grace's reaction. She cleared her throat, capturing his attention once more.

"As it happens, the horse was spooked *because* of Mr. Hondros," she said. "And then, wouldn't you know it, but I saw him again just that night."

"Oh, it was destiny!" Mrs. Mulberry said, clapping her hands together excitedly.

"Or something else entirely," Grace said with some ice in her tone. "It was at the boxing match Father took us to."

"Oh, I do hate those matches, don't you, Mr. Hondros? Although," her face fell as she realized what Grace was saying, "I suppose if you were present, you must enjoy it as much as my husband does."

"It is more of a business matter for me, Mrs. Mulberry," Damien said, proud of his smooth delivery.

"I see," she said, nodding sagely, although Damien could tell that she had no idea at all what he was talking about — and rightly so.

"Mother," Grace broke in, "would it be all right if I had a moment to speak with Mr. Hondros alone? We shall leave the door to the drawing room open."

"Of course," her mother said, standing now and beaming once more. "I will return in a few minutes."

Damien stood, nodding his thankfulness, his eyes on the woman's back as she walked out the door. For the truth was, as much as he appreciated a moment on his own with Grace, he was equally as frightened for just what she was going to say once the two of them were alone.

* * *

"Grace," he said lightly once he resumed his seat, and Grace arched her brows in response, speaking before he could continue.

"Now that my mother is gone, perhaps you would like to tell me what you are really doing here."

"Of course," he said, far too composed for her liking. Was he always like this? Never showing his true emotion but rather just the exterior? "I came to apologize."

"For what?"

As much as she had been frightened off by his display of violence last night, Grace was well aware that he had done nothing wrong — he had behaved as he always did, had simply done his job. It was *she* who had run away, because the man she had thought she was falling for was nothing at all as she had imagined him to be. It wasn't Damien's fault that she had built him into a man he wasn't — it was her own. She knew he fought for a living. Why would she assume he only did so in the boxing ring?

"For whatever happened that drove you away last night."

"I simply had to go."

"You left your brother behind."

She waved a hand in the air, even as she refused to look him in the eye.

"Borden was likely there all night. I would likely have fallen fast asleep waiting for him."

"You wouldn't be the first at the establishment to do so."

Grace didn't answer that, not wanting to think about what it might mean.

"But I promise I would have kept you awake."

Damien leaned in toward her, tentatively extending a hand, but Grace couldn't bring herself to reach out and take it, yet nor could she lift her own away and out of his grasp. In the end, she allowed his fingertips to hover against hers with the gentlest of touches, for she wasn't wearing gloves now. Despite all that had already occurred between them, the light caress still gave her shivers.

"What are you doing?" she whispered.

"I'm still thinking about that... dance," he said in a low voice, even though Grace was aware of what he truly meant by that. "Did you leave because you saw how I handled those men?"

Grace paused, wanting to lie, to tell him no, that had nothing to do with it, but instead, she found herself nodding slowly. "I did."

"I understand," he said, pulling his hand back as he retreated within himself, and Grace could feel the loss of his touch as much as it had filled her with an unexplained joy. "This might be difficult to believe, but I am not, by my nature, a violent person. I just..." He seemed to be having difficulty explaining himself. "I do it to keep peace at such an event, to prevent anyone else from getting hurt. I do it to protect."

Grace bit her lip. She supposed she could somewhat understand that, but she still wished it could be left up to someone else. He did not seem to truly be a hot-tempered man, and yet in the course of a week she had already seen him use his fists and his body as his greatest method of communication — twice.

"But why do you have to do it?" she asked softly, looking up at him imploringly.

Damien shrugged, staring off at a painting of a fruit basket, rubbing his chin at the question as though he had never thought particularly hard about it before. "Because I'm good at it."

"Have you always been? For how long?" Suddenly she wanted nothing more than to learn all she could about him, but he shifted his body away from her, as though hiding this part of himself.

"I brought you something," he said in a lighter tone, changing the subject entirely, which bothered her, but now was not the time to protest. Grace sensed if she pushed any harder, he might never open up to her again.

"You didn't have to do that."

"I know," he said, pulling a long box out of his jacket. "My brother and his wife own a jewellery shop."

"They do?" she asked, surprised, but then immediately suspicion intervened. "Is it… ah…"

"Legitimate? Yes," he said with a smile. "It is all legal, with no ill-gotten goods. I would never give you something stolen."

He held the box out to her. "I saw this and I… thought of you."

A sudden rush of color entered his cheeks, and Grace had to hold back her smile at his bashfulness.

While she was well aware that accepting a gift from a man was all but accepting his offer for something to develop between them, she couldn't help her curiosity.

She took the box from him, even as she knew she shouldn't, cracking it open to peer within.

And gasped.

"Oh, Damien," she breathed with admiration. "It's beautiful."

With hesitant fingers, she reached in and felt the delicate chain of the necklace, pulling it out to stare at the bold, beautiful hanging ruby with some wonder. Her father had always been generous with gifts for his children, but his gifts had always been practical, like quill pens and new boots. Nothing like this, something that held such beauty, and given for no reason at all.

"Do you like it?" he asked somewhat trepidatiously, and Grace looked up with a similar tremulous smile.

"I love it," she said, before staring back at it regretfully. "But I cannot accept it."

He practically recoiled, stricken at her words. "Why not?"

"Because, it's… it's not right for me to take something like this from you. I am more than appreciative, I truly am, and am so pleased that you thought of me, but… I just cannot."

"What do you mean, you *cannot*?"

Grace closed her eyes as her mother's voice thundered in from the doorway.

"Mother, I thought you were waiting outside," she said through gritted teeth as her mother stormed into the room.

"I was, but I couldn't help overhearing that last bit as I was returning. Now, Mr. Hondros has been quite generous to you, and for you to turn away his gift would be the height of rudeness."

"Mother, I—"

But as always, her mother was not to be ignored. Grace had spent most of her life being drowned out by her mother, who she loved dearly though she was certainly overbearing. Her brothers had always managed to avoid her commanding ways, but Grace often had no other choice.

In this, however, she had to remain strong.

"In fact, if you will *not* accept it, I just might have to do so in your stead!"

Her mother laughed at that as Damien managed a weak smile, although he seemed just as perplexed regarding how to handle this as Grace was. Grace just sighed. With her mother, she always found it best to allow her to have her way for the moment and then Grace did as she pleased later on.

"Very well," she said. "I accept. Thank you, Mr. Hondros, for your generosity and thoughtfulness."

Although she wanted to add that it didn't change anything.

But something else most certainly would.

Another presence filled the doorway — one as forceful as her mother, but much louder.

"Damien Hondros — what the hell are you doing in my home?"

CHAPTER 9

Damien had hoped that, perhaps, if he were to run into Arthur Mulberry, the man might not recognize him outside of the boxing ring.

He had been sorely mistaken.

"Mr. Mulberry," he said, standing, aware of Grace and her mother, both who seemed momentarily frozen, unsure of just how to react to Mulberry's vehemence.

Grace's mother recovered first.

"Arthur, Mr. Hondros is a guest of Grace's. Perhaps we should—"

"Perhaps we should nothing!" Mulberry stormed into the room, his ire obviously growing with each step toward Damien. "Do you know who this man is?"

"A friend of Grace's," Mrs. Mulberry repeated, not realizing that her words were having the opposite effect she intended.

"A friend of Grace's," Mulberry repeated, scorn in his tone. "He's also a liar and a fraud and a thief!"

"Oh, now I'm sure that isn't true," Mrs. Mulberry said, although she looked at Damien with new doubt in her eyes.

"Father," Grace began. "I really don't think—"

"It doesn't matter what you think! It matters that you stand up for this family."

Damien crossed his arms over his chest. Mulberry might be Grace's father, but he didn't like the idea of anyone speaking to her like that — no one at all.

"As it happens, Mr. Mulberry," Damien said, his slow, calm, yet icy tone cutting through the room, "I came to see Grace but also have a package to leave for you."

"Oh?" Mulberry didn't seem completely mollified, but he was obviously interested in whatever Damien had to offer.

"I understand that you felt cheated from the fight the other night. Of course, with fights and gambling, there is never any guarantee that one party is going to come away victorious. However, as a gesture of goodwill and to prove that I am serious about my interest in seeing more of Grace — and your family — I would like to offer you the money I won from the fight, which should be nearly equal to that which you put down on it."

Mulberry eyed him suspiciously, but did not hesitate in taking the offering out of Damien's hand.

"I'm not sure I understand your intentions here."

"It means more to me to have an amiable relationship with you than it does to have the money."

"Why?"

Damien furrowed his brow. How did the man not yet understand? "Because of Grace."

Grace looked as equally dumbfounded as her father, and he could not understand why the entire family seemed so confused.

He took a breath before saying it again, slowly. "I would like to have the opportunity to spend more time with Grace." He turned to her, allowing her the opportunity to choose. "If you would so wish it."

She stared right back at him, neither of them looking to either of her parents, although Damien could sense her mother sighing somewhat dreamily as she watched them with her hands clasped in front of her while Mulberry still exuded an air of disapproval.

"I..." Grace began, seemingly still unsure, "I suppose that we could see what might come of it."

"I am glad to hear it," Damien said, unable to help the grin from breaking out across his face as he anticipated more time spent with her. "Perhaps a visit tomorrow?"

"Come for dinner," Mulberry interjected, and Damien turned to him slowly.

"For dinner?"

"Yes," Mulberry said, a suspicious grin sliding over his face. "With the family. Then we can... get to know you better."

"Very well," Damien said, swallowing hard. "Dinner it is."

* * *

"WILL YOU COME, LYDIA, PLEASE?"

Grace knew that she should be able to face a dinner with her family and one single man on her own. But she would far prefer to have some support.

Lydia folded her arms over her chest and looked at Grace from her seat across from her on the sofa of the Campbell's sitting room. Their townhouse was not nearly as lavish as Grace's, but it was comfortable, and Grace often felt more at home here than she did in her father's townhouse.

"Don't you think it would be rather odd for me to attend a family dinner when you are supposed to be entertaining the man who would like to court you?"

Grace made a face.

"I don't like that word. It makes me feel like I am some genteel young lady from a high-born family."

Lydia heaved a sigh. "Very well. What would you like to call it then?"

"I suppose the man who would like to spend time with me?"

"Before we discuss dinner, Grace, perhaps we should address the more pressing matter."

"Which is?"

"Do you *want* to *spend time* with him? What would you like to get out of this? You literally ran away from him the other night!"

Grace looked down forlornly at the cup in her hand. "I don't know. I suppose if he was just the man I met at the bookshop, then yes, of course. But he is more than that. There is so much to him, to his family, that I don't know. And what I have seen, I have not particularly enjoyed."

"You cannot change him."

"I am aware of that," Grace said with a nod. "But whether or not I can accept all of him… I just don't know. I suppose that is what I would like to find out."

"While having some fun along the way," Lydia added with a sly grin, and Grace pretended to throw a biscuit at her at the comment.

"There is also the other question…"

"Which is?"

"Why would he want anything to do with me? My father has been outright boorish to him, I haven't been the most accepting of him, and I certainly don't have much else to offer."

"That is entirely untrue, Grace Mulberry, and for you to say so is insulting to me."

"What have you got to do with this?"

"Well, I am your closest of friends, am I not? If you are

such a terrible person, then what does that say about me and my choice of companions?"

Grace opened her mouth in astonishment, unsure of how to respond, until Lydia began to laugh.

"Oh, Grace, your face. I am just teasing. But in truth, you must know that you are the kindest, most generous, most intelligent person that I know and for you to think any differently is preposterous. You are also one of the most beautiful, and I won't have you saying anything to the contrary."

"But—"

"Ah!" Lydia held up a finger. "Not allowed. Perhaps you are not the most classic of beauties — nor am I — but there is an essence about you that is absolutely delightful and when you smile, the entire room lights up. People feel comfortable with you, accepted, and that means more than anything else ever could. Now I realize that I *have* to come in order to ensure that you actually show up for this dinner. Tell me, what time should I be there?"

* * *

"You are having dinner with her family already?" Arie rubbed his hands together. "This is excellent news."

"Arie—"

But Arie wasn't listening. He was already pacing the floor of the sitting room as Damien, Diana, Xander, and Juliet looked on.

"You won't get anything out of Mulberry, not at first. He still doesn't trust you. Perhaps one of the sons. Borden can sometimes have too much liquor, while Jeremiah is the one who is most open, I'd say. Don't know anything about the third brother, but he's not even in London. Yes, Jeremiah. He's the one. Try to get close to him, ask a few questions for more information, although nothing that will have him questioning your motives for being there. Can you do that?"

"What of the poor girl?" Juliet broke in. Xander's wife had been on the other end of such a scheme before and obviously didn't care for the deception. As it happened, Damien wasn't feeling overly comfortable about this either.

"I'm hoping that Grace never finds out about any of this," Damien muttered.

"And if she does?" Juliet challenged. "How will you explain it?"

Damien had always liked Juliet, but she had a propensity for asking the difficult questions.

Damien scratched his forehead.

"Arie, you want to work with her father, correct?"

Arie nodded.

"The fact of the matter is, I am not using Grace. I would like to see her, whether or not Arie has an interest in her family's business. If my becoming closer to her leads to a partnership, that can only be a good thing, can it not? A bonus, if you will?"

Juliet stood up from her seat next to Xander and stepped up to Damien, her arms crossed and one eyebrow crooked.

"Damien," she said, softer now. "You are a good man. But you must ask yourself — who are you trying to convince right now — me? Or yourself?"

Silence filled the air around them until Diana stood, smoothing out her dress as she surveyed the room.

"I hate to interrupt, but Calli and the children will be here for dinner at any moment."

Not only did Calli's presence mean that business dealings — as legitimate as they were — were not to be discussed, but most discussion became nearly impossible when she arrived with her eight-year-old niece and nephew and one-year-old daughter.

Damien heaved a sigh of relief, pleased that they would be leaving the discussion alone.

Of course Juliet didn't miss his expression, as she pointed a finger at him.

"Don't get too excited," she said with a stern look. "We're not done this conversation quite yet."

As much as Damien was looking forward to seeing Grace, he had to admit that he was starting to wonder — was he making a big mistake?

CHAPTER 10

There were many things that made Grace nervous.

Entering a room full of people she didn't know.

Being left to speak to a man her mother had just introduced her to.

Thinking about the future and what would be waiting for her if she never got married.

But she had never realized just how much trepidation one simple dinner could cause.

Her mother had entered her bedroom a few times now to remind her not to be late – which was one bad habit that Grace was all too aware of regarding herself.

She would, however, be on time tonight, if only to ensure that Damien, her father, and brothers were not left alone together for an overly long period of time.

That could spell disaster.

In fact, the entire evening could be a complete catastrophe if she wasn't careful. It would have to be a careful walk between not allowing any over-enthusiasm and keeping her wits about her to prevent anyone from coming to blows.

Although it was obvious who would win if that occurred.

"Grace, Lydia is here!"

Thank goodness. Grace had purposely told her friend to arrive a few minutes early, to help her face what was to come. Grace knew she owed Lydia for this, but she hadn't yet thought of how she was going to pay her back.

"Is there anything else you need?" Maria, maid to both Grace and her mother looked at her inquiringly in the mirror. Grace had chosen an emerald green silk gown tonight, one that she knew was rather becoming on her. "Any jewellery, perhaps?" Grace's mother, upon one of her many visits, had not been subtle in expressing her desire for Grace to wear the necklace that Damien had given her, but Grace was hesitant about sending the wrong message. She didn't want him to read too much into the action.

But in the end, she couldn't help the way it pulled at her from the top of her vanity.

"Oh, very well, best put it on."

Maria smiled approvingly before fastening the clasp around Grace's neck.

"Beautiful. As are you, Miss."

Grace nodded her thanks before she stood, squared her shoulders, and started downstairs to greet whatever was before her. When she descended, she could hear the chatter of voices in the drawing room beyond, and she stopped in the doorway, surprised to find that her entire family had made themselves available this evening. It was seldom that all of her brothers came home at the same time. Her eldest brother, Max, was usually away in Dover overseeing the family's shipping interests there, while Borden was the one who made new connections for the family here in London. Jeremiah was her only brother still living at home.

Lydia was, surprisingly, leaning against the fireplace, a drink in her hand as she stared up at Borden, laughing at something he had said. Grace paused. That was Lydia's flirting laugh. But she couldn't be flirting with… Borden. Could she?

Grace was so caught up in analyzing what was occurring in front of her that she didn't realize she wasn't alone until the last possible moment.

"They seem to be getting along rather well, do they not?"

Grace jumped before placing a hand over her heart as she turned to stare at the solid wall of linen-clad muscle behind her.

"Damien. You startled me."

"My apologies. I thought the butler would have announced me."

"Ah. Well, he can be rather… suspect."

Damien nodded, amusement on his face, and Grace turned around quickly before she could become too enamoured with his expression.

"You didn't have to agree to this," she murmured.

"Why wouldn't I?" he asked, his breath softly brushing against her ear, and Grace had to still her body from trembling at its feather-light touch. "I wanted to spend time with you. What better way to get to know you than to have dinner with your family?"

"Well, you will know once you've *spent* the entire evening with my family," she said wryly. "I love them, but they can be… an acquired taste."

"I know the feeling," he said, laughter in his voice before he held his elbow out toward her. "Shall we?"

She nodded, tentatively placing her hand on his sleeve, wondering what her family would say about them entering the room together.

She didn't have long to conjecture, as most conversation in the room ceased once her family became aware of their presence.

Fortunately, silence didn't long reign when her mother was in the room.

"Mr. Hondros!" she exclaimed, sailing across the expanse of garish red carpet toward them. "How wonderful to see you again!"

The rest of her family didn't seem to be quite as enthusiastic, which Grace understood. Her father had made it quite clear that this dinner was being held with the purpose of convincing Grace that seeing Damien again was not in anyone's best interests — not her family's, nor hers, which apparently he felt were one and the same.

Her mother had been the one to stand up for Damien of course, although why she was so enthusiastic about him, Grace wasn't entirely certain. If she had to guess, it was likely that her mother had given up on any other prospect for Grace, and was willing to consider that Damien was the best — and only — potential for Grace to ever find someone to take care of her.

"Thank you for having me," Damien said with a nod to the family. Borden nodded back, his suspicion obvious, while Max and Jeremiah seemed much more intrigued by the entire situation.

"Glad to have you here," Jeremiah said, only to receive his father's displeased stare. Jeremiah just shrugged, obviously as uncaring as he usually was about such things.

"Come in, come in, and we will get you something to drink. What do you like?" Grace's mother asked, while her father added, "we've no shortage of anything," rather proudly, and suddenly Grace realized that her father likely had a secondary reason to ask Damien here — so that he could show off his wealth. Why it mattered, she had no idea. Her father was in shipping. How did that have anything to do with Damien's work — in boxing or in protecting his brother's business interests?

As Damien accepted a glass of amber liquid from her father, Grace tried to slink away into the shadows of the room next to Lydia, who seemed rather intrigued by the entire situation despite her initial reluctance to attend.

"Your mother has quite the penchant for Damien Hondros, doesn't she?" Lydia asked with a quirk of her lips, to which Grace sighed.

"I believe my mother would likely 'have a penchant' for anyone who would show the slightest bit of interest in me," she said wryly.

"Well, he *is* good looking, in his own way," Lydia said, causing the slightest twinge of jealousy to rise in Grace's belly, which was ridiculous. She was simply enjoying her time with Damien, and Lydia had no designs on him, nor would she ever due to her loyalty to Grace.

"Speaking of interest," Grace said, unable to keep her eyes from Damien as he crossed the room to speak to her brother, Jeremiah — a good choice as he was the friendliest and most harmless of them all. "What were you and Borden discussing?"

"Me and Borden?" Lydia asked, her eyes widening innocently. "Nothing at all. Just the usual frivolities."

"I see," Grace said, too distracted to pursue it any further at the moment. She tried to convince herself that it was just her own wandering, romantic mind that was telling stories and that there was nothing of which she should be overly suspect. "What do you think Jeremiah and Damien are talking about?"

"I don't know," Lydia said, laughter in her voice, "but why don't you go find out?"

"Find out?"

"Yes! Walk over there and join the conversation."

"Oh, but I couldn't. I just—"

Lydia chuckled softly before giving Grace the slightest of pushes on the small of her back. "Just go."

* * *

DAMIEN WAS DISCOVERING that the youngest son of the Mulberry family was much more forthcoming than he could ever have imagined. He was mid-description of the base of their operations in Dover when Grace joined the conversation.

While her timing was perhaps not ideal when considering Arie's motivations for him being here, Damien couldn't help his pleasure that she, at least, seemed to want to speak to him.

"Gracie," Jeremiah said with a grin, "nice of you to introduce Hondros here to the family. He's a good man. Much better than Father would ever let us believe."

"Jeremiah!" she exclaimed, before turning to Damien with horror on her face. "I'm so sorry. He didn't mean—"

"It's fine," Damien said, holding up a hand. "I know our families have not gotten off to the best of beginnings. I am, however, hoping to change that and am happy to be here tonight."

Grace nodded, and Damien couldn't resist looking down at her neck to see the ruby that was nestled between her breasts. When her face immediately flushed, he realized that she had mistaken his gaze.

"The necklace looks lovely on you," he said in part-apology. "I couldn't help but admire it."

"Oh, thank you," she said, bringing her hand to it immediately. "Well, of course, thank *you*. As it was because of you – oh, you know what I mean."

Damien nodded, wishing he didn't make her so flustered.

His brother Xander always knew how to make a woman feel more at ease, but he, unfortunately, lacked such skills. Women came to him because they were impressed by his strength and power, not because he wooed them with his words.

Fortunately, Jeremiah soon took over the conversation once more, only to be interrupted by Mulberry himself, who seemed to suddenly realize that his son was, perhaps, oversharing.

"Let's go in to dinner," he said, pointing to the other room, despite Mrs. Mulberry's immediate protests that dinner would not yet be ready.

"We can't!" she said, practically flying after him. "Not yet! The cook will not be pleased. I told her we would be another hour, and now you are—"

"In to dinner," he said tersely. "The cook works for us, does she not?"

"Well, yes, of course, but—"

"Then she will accommodate us."

Mrs. Mulberry placed a hand over her forehead in despair, but followed her husband into the room, immediately changing tactics as she smiled apologetically at the rest of them.

Damien didn't offer Grace his arm this time, but was pleased when she walked beside him and sat next to him at the table.

"So tell me," he said lowly, for her ears only, "do you have a place in the family business?"

"No." She shook her head. "I have offered to keep the accounts before, but my father won't hear of it. He says the business has no place for a woman's involvement. I have tried to tell him many times that I am just as smart as my brothers and even received much of the same initial education, but he is not one to be reasoned with."

She looked around so furtively that he nearly laughed.

"Although you probably already know that," she continued. "I am sorry that he took your money. You earned it."

Damien shrugged. "I just hope that it will help broker some peace between us."

"He was the one who chose to gamble it," she said, shaking her head. "Gambled money is no sure thing."

"True," Damien said with a shrug. "But it's no matter."

Before she could question him any further, the harried maid and housekeeper ran in with the first course — fish cooked in wine from Bordeaux, Mr. Mulberry was quick to tell them. Grace's family were fairly well off by middle class means, running the household on a small staff — butler, housekeeper, cook, footman, driver, and maid. Grace's mother would have liked to hire on more, but her father had always said that they had more than enough for appearances.

Talk around the table ran to every day mundane matters, the little conversation topics that Grace always hated. She far preferred to discuss real matters with people she knew well, rather than trivial items or gossip that only served to fill the silence.

But for tonight, trivial matters would be just fine.

"So tell us, Mr. Hondros, what do you do for a living?"

Perhaps the thought had crossed Grace's mind far too soon. She looked at her mother in supplication, trying to shake her head to steer her attention in a different direction, but her mother had never picked up on the art of subtlety.

"Well," Damien began slowly, placing his fork down beside his plate, striking Grace with the impression that Damien never did anything that wasn't deliberate. "As you know, I am a boxer."

Grace's father snorted at that, causing glares to be sent his way from both Grace and her mother.

"You cannot make a living off of that, can you?" Grace's father asked snidely, but Damien just shook his head.

"No, I cannot. I do not fight often enough to do so. I also help my brother with some of his business interests."

"Ah, yes, tell us more of the Hondros business interests," her father said, and Grace began to pray in earnest that they would change topics.

"He owns a gaming hell," Damien began. "I make sure that everything runs smoothly. That there are no complications."

"Using the same skills that you do in the boxing ring?" Borden asked, sitting back with his arms crossed.

"Sometimes," Damien said without showing any hint of annoyance at the question.

"Well, one thing is for sure," Jeremiah said with a laugh, "we can trust him to keep our sister safe!"

Grace swallowed. This was going to be a long night.

CHAPTER 11

"Did you acquire any information?" Arie asked the moment Damien walked through the door, and Damien continued past him, rolling his eyes when he had turned from Arie's view.

"As a matter of fact, I did," Damien said, removing his cloak and hanging it on a hook in the entrance. "I learned that Grace is not like anyone else in her family, save, perhaps, the eldest brother who lives in Dover. He's the quiet sort, who listens rather than speaks. I learned that her father is still overly suspicious of me. And I learned that the shipping company primarily deals in textiles, most notably silks and lace, but also tea, and brandy. And maybe some chocolate."

"Why didn't you lead with that?" Arie asked, walking past Damien, rubbing his hands together. "How much of the business is legitimate?"

"I have no idea," Damien said, holding his hands up in the air. "But I would guess less than half from what Jeremiah said. Most of the product is brought in through the arm of the company based in Dover — which the eldest, Max, looks after. It is also, interestingly, where the family has a second home."

"*Very* interesting," Arie's eyes gleamed. "I don't suppose you could find yourself an invitation?"

"I just met the woman," Damien said wryly. "I don't think they're going to be inviting me to join the family for the summer quite yet."

Arie shrugged. "One never knows."

"How was the dinner itself, Damien?"

The brothers turned to find Diana had quietly entered the room behind them. Her question seemed rather sincere, as though she was truly interested in how Damien's evening had gone. Diana was surprising. Sometimes the side of her emerged that was much more caring than what she most often allowed others to see.

"It was… interesting," Damien said slowly. "I think Grace was happy to have me there, although there were moments I could tell she was questioning the evening — as I was myself, now and again. They were quite interested in your business, Arie, but I was sure to keep my answers vague, obviously. Grace's mother was practically throwing her daughter at me, and her father maintained his suspicion. But," he contemplated, "by the time I said goodnight, which was not long after a cigar and a brandy with Mulberry and his sons, I was invited to return, so that must be a good sign, is it not?"

"I'd say so," said Diana with a small smile. "I don't see how any woman in the world wouldn't welcome you into her life, Damien."

Damien gave a small chuckle. "There seems to be one woman who has her doubts," he said, rubbing his forehead. "And she's the only one who seems to matter anymore."

* * *

"GRACE! COME HERE!"

Grace looked up from her book, perplexed at where the bellow had come from. She was rather comfortable, lounging in the window seat — her reading nook — in the corner of the drawing room.

Her mother frowned from her position on the settee, one needle poised in the air.

"Was that your father?"

"I wasn't aware he was home," Grace said dryly. "Usually everyone in the house knows when he has arrived."

"Best go see what he wants," her mother said with a sigh.

"Must I?" Grace asked, burrowing deeper into the soft cushions below her. "Perhaps I could pretend that I am out."

"It will never work, dear," her mother said apologetically. "Trust me, I've tried."

"Very well," Grace said, spinning to plant her feet on the floor before heading down the hall to her father's study. She was surprised to find him already walking down the corridor.

"Father. Good afternoon."

"Grace, come to my study. I must have a word with you."

"Oh?"

Grace's father never invited her into his study. His study was for business which, he had always made abundantly clear, was not a place for women — especially his daughter.

"I've been thinking," he began, and Grace inwardly cringed. When her father began thinking, he was usually coming up with some idea or another, and she wasn't sure that she wanted one of those ideas to include her.

"Yes?"

"Do you still want to help with the accounts for the business?"

Grace started in surprise.

"You'd like *me* to help with the accounts?"

"Our current bookkeeper is no longer with us, and I need some help until I can find someone who would suit," he said. "I can obviously trust you, and while I would have to have someone else oversee the more detailed accounts of course, you could help."

Grace tried to ignore the slight that she couldn't handle the entirety of the business. She supposed the best thing to do would be to agree to whatever her father offered her and then prove herself from there.

"Whatever you need, Father," she said with a demure smile, not wanting to appear overeager. "I am happy to help."

"Good," he said with a nod. "Borden will give you all of the particulars later today. You won't let me down, will you, Grace?"

"Of course not, Father," she said. "Thank you."

He nodded. "There's something else."

"Oh?"

"Hondros."

"What about him?" Grace asked warily. While last night's dinner had gone slightly better than expected, Grace's expectations had been fairly low to begin with, knowing her family as well as their history with Damien's. That they had managed to finish the dinner without anyone coming to blows of any sort was just short of miraculous, but there were still more than a few barbed insults that Grace didn't particularly care for.

"Be careful with him," her father said. "He might be a better man than his brother, but that is not saying much. He's still a fighter, and he's still from unknown origins. I don't trust him."

"Not to worry, Father. I'm always careful," Grace promised, and her father surprised her by reaching out and ruffling her hair as though she was still a child.

"Good girl," he said with a nod before returning to the ledgers, dismissing her.

Grace rose and left the room, although not without a look behind her, curious at just what that was all about.

* * *

"So you will be working with Borden?"

Grace eyed Lydia suspiciously at which part of her story she seemed most interested in. "Yes. He didn't seem particularly thrilled about it, but Father didn't give him much choice."

"I see," Lydia said, looking to the side as though she had no further interest in the subject, but Grace knew better.

"Lydia," she said, keeping her tone light, "when did your interest in Borden begin?"

Lydia gasped, turning toward her as she placed a hand over her heart dramatically. "I have no interest in your brother!"

"Oh, Lydia, there is no reason to lie to me," Grace said with a small smile. "I know you better than you perhaps know yourself."

Lydia paused for a moment as though trying to determine what she could get away with before finally sighing. "Very well. Borden… well, you know, Grace, since I have no siblings of my own, I have always considered your brothers to be very like mine as well."

Grace nodded. Lydia was right. That was how it had always been.

"Then, somewhere along the way, I don't know what happened. Borden just became more… attractive somehow. I think it all began the night we went to that masquerade party, when I saw him with other women. I didn't like it, and after that, I found myself trying to make him jealous. I couldn't see him as a brother any longer, but as something more."

"Does he feel the same about you?" Grace asked, stepping behind Lydia for a moment to allow a family to pass by them as they walked down Compton Street.

"I don't know!" Lydia said somewhat desperately, with none of her usual composure. "What do you think?"

Grace shrugged. "Borden is not a man who can be easily read," she said. "He is nothing like Father or Mother, but rather has his own way of seeing things. Ways that he keeps to himself. He knows how to be charming, yet there is more to him that he doesn't let many see."

"I know," Lydia said morosely. "I see it, but I don't know how to make him see the same. I want to learn more about him. I can't help but find myself hoping for more. I have no idea if he feels any of the same."

Grace was silent for a moment, mulling over these new revelations, until Lydia began tugging on her arm.

"Grace, there he is!"

"Borden?" Grace asked, wondering what Borden was doing outside the shipping yard. It was to where they were currently walking, and now Grace knew why Lydia had been so insistent on accompanying her. She had told Grace that she was bored, but she obviously wanted to see Borden.

"Not Borden. Damien!"

"Damien?" Grace said in confusion. "What would Damien be doing here?"

Lydia shrugged, clearly as lost as Grace, but while Grace had slowed her step at finding Damien ahead of her, Lydia tugged on her arm, pulling her closer.

"Wait," Grace hissed, "we should see what he is doing here first."

"Grace, the man would like to court you. There is no reason to avoid him!"

"I hate that word," Grace grumbled as Lydia rolled her eyes at her, obviously not caring in the least.

"Mr. Hondros!" Lydia called out, waving her arm around so enthusiastically that despite Grace's attempts to pull it down, he would have no option but to see them coming.

Grace forced a smile on her face, even as she looked down to remember just what she was wearing. Her pale pink dress. Right. Not her finest, but it would do.

"Miss Mulberry. And Miss Campbell," Damien greeted them as they drew near. "Lovely to see you."

"What are you doing here?" Grace blurted out before she could stop herself, Lydia's gaze as searing as her own self-admonishment.

"I came to see your brother, actually," Damien said, and Grace furrowed her brow.

"Borden?"

"Jeremiah, actually," Damien said. "We have a few common interests, and I thought he might be interested in further conversation."

"I see," Grace said, even though she didn't at all. From what she had gathered, Damien and Jeremiah'd had a brief conversation, but she had no idea what could possibly be common between them besides an acquaintance with her. Lydia, however, was nodding at her encouragingly as though this was a positive sign.

"Oh, look, I see Borden crossing through the yard," Lydia said, not at all subtly. "Perhaps I'd best go and greet him. I'll leave the two of you to join us in a moment."

She was only a few steps away when Damien began to chuckle. "She is rather like your mother."

"Like my mother?" Grace repeated, horrified.

"Yes," Damien said, "when it comes to seeing you matched off, at least."

Grace looked down to hide what she was sure was

redness in her cheeks, wondering if she could pass it off due to the exertion of her walk or the warmth of the day. When she looked up at Damien's slightly teasing grin, however, she had a feeling that he wasn't fooled.

"I have a confession to make," Damien said, clasping his hands behind his back. "I am here to see Jeremiah because I was hoping that he could help bring me closer to you."

"Oh?" Grace lifted a brow.

Damien shrugged one shoulder, looking off into the distance. "I thought it wouldn't hurt to have a member of your family in support of me, and he seemed the most likely candidate."

"Besides my mother," Grace added wryly, to which Damien laughed.

"Yes, besides your mother."

"Well, as it happens, I've never put much stock in Jeremiah's opinions as they seem to change daily," she said. "Borden and Max are much more reliable, although one can never be sure just what Borden is thinking."

"So it seems," Damien said. "I cannot tell if he approves of me or not."

"It is not really for him to decide," Grace said, biting her lip, unsure if this could be called flirting or not. If it could, she had no idea whether or not she was blundering it.

"Your father, then?" Damien asked, and Grace squared her shoulders and looked up at him.

"I decide what is best for me," she said, before laughing lightly, "although both my father and mother would likely say otherwise."

Damien chuckled at that, capturing the attention of some of the workers in the yard, who were unloading one of the shipments recently arrived from Dover.

"What brings you here today?" he asked. "Do you often visit the family business?"

"No," she said, brightening at the reminder of the responsibility she had recently been entrusted with. "As it happens, my father has finally come round and asked me to help with some of the accounts. I'm to learn more from Borden this afternoon."

"Good for you," Damien said, although Grace could have sworn she saw a look of regret flash over his eyes. Why would it matter to him? Was he one of those men who thought women should do nothing but sit on the sofa and practice needlepoint?

"I'm attending a lecture tonight across the street from The British Museum," Grace said, unsure even as the words came out of her mouth just why she was saying them. "Would you like to join me?"

Damien seemed as surprised as she but he nodded, his eyes burning into her in a way that promised, perhaps, more than the lecture to come.

"I would love nothing more," he said before reaching out, squeezing her hand, and walking away without another glance behind him, leaving Grace more perplexed than ever about this enigma of a man.

CHAPTER 12

Damien cautiously entered the lecture hall, unsure of exactly what to expect. He had seen the building before, but had never actually entered — he'd never had a reason to do so. Arie had made sure they had received rudimentary schooling — he had eventually hired a tutor for them once he could afford it — but Damien had never been as adept as Diana or even Xander or Calli. Lessons took longer to come to him, and while he always enjoyed reading and the stories available on the pages of a book, he assumed lectures such as these were far above anything he could ever follow.

But Grace had invited him, and he would agree to anything if it was at her request.

He had no idea what was becoming of him — he was never such a man who based his comings and goings on the whims of a woman — but he was drawn to her like a gambler to a faro table.

The room was set up in rows of chairs, and while Damien received a few curious glances, most of the attendees simply looked at him and away as though he was of no consequence. How different a crowd than what he was used to.

He immediately found Grace, sitting near the back of the room, her posture straight and her hands in her lap. He was both pleased and horrified to find that she was alone.

"Where is Lydia? Your brothers?" he asked as he sat down next to her, before he had even greeted her.

"I came alone," she whispered back, the answering volume of her voice making it clear that he should lower his. "Our footman accompanied me and is waiting outside."

Damien frowned, although he had to admit that he was somewhat pleased he had been considered a worthy candidate for such an event.

A thin, bespectacled man soon made his way to the front of the room, opening a book on the lectern in front of him, and Damien realized that he had no idea what the topic of this lecture even was.

Soon, however, it became clear. Mathematics, of some sort that he couldn't quite make out.

Damien nearly groaned aloud. He knew absolutely nothing of the subject nor did he have any desire to. Grace, however, was giving the speaker her rapt attention. Damien decided that it would be best to enjoy the hour — for surely this could not go on for more than an hour as how much could one say about mathematics? — enjoying watching Grace's reactions. She was more animated than he had seen her through nearly their entire acquaintance.

After a time, the speaker began to ask questions of the crowd. A few men shouted out answers, as Grace mumbled nearly beneath her breath.

"What was that?" Damien asked, and Grace turned to him in surprise, as though not even realizing she had said anything.

"Nothing."

"You were answering him," Damien said, "and it seems as though your answers were correct."

Grace flushed. "Perhaps. I have read a bit about this area of mathematics before, including the book he is currently referring to."

"Well, answer him — aloud," Damien encouraged, and she shook her head.

"I couldn't."

"Why not?"

"These men would never accept my answers."

"You'll never know until you try."

They received a few looks as they were obviously interrupting the listeners around them, but when the speaker asked a question again, Grace took a quick, trepidatious look at Damien before tentatively calling out the answer.

She wasn't heard, but the answer was shortly proven to be correct.

Damien beamed, proud of her in a strange way he couldn't explain.

The next time Grace answered a little louder, a little braver, and the speaker nodded to her, his bushy brows rising in surprise.

"Correct, Miss," he said, and Grace finally allowed a small smile to emerge.

The lecture seemed to be over so quickly that Damien couldn't entirely remember just why he had been so averse to it. It had actually proven to be much more enjoyable than he ever would have imagined — although it was obviously the company and not the subject that had made it so.

"Can I accompany you home?" he asked, unsure of how exactly to play the part of a gentleman. Usually when he accompanied a woman home, the ending was altogether different from what this night would be.

Grace hesitated. "Best not. I told Father that I was meeting Lydia."

"I could leave you near your door."

"The footman would say something," she said, although Damien hoped that was regret in her voice. "He is most loyal to Father."

"Very well," Damien said as they stood outside the building in the darkness of night. "Thank you for inviting me. I had a surprisingly very enjoyable time — surprising because of the subject, and not the company."

Grace laughed lightly, a sound that caused tingles to race down Damien's spine and for all of the hairs on his arm to stand on end.

"As did I."

"When will I see you again?"

"Hopefully soon," she said, looking up at him from beneath her lashes, and Damien wanted nothing more in that moment than to pull her toward him and take her lips with his. What would she taste like? He imagined plush berries and juicy peaches — why, he had no idea. Perhaps Diana was right and he *had* been reading too many novels.

"Where is your footman?" he asked, not wanting to relinquish her in the dark of night even with a man accompanying her. As it happened, he wasn't particularly thrilled that someone else had been tasked with protecting her.

"He's waiting just up there, in that alcove," she said, pointing ahead. "I would have taken the carriage, but it's only a few minutes' walk."

Damien nodded, lifting her gloved hand in his and placing a gentle kiss upon it so that it was clear what his intentions were.

"Good night, then, Grace."

"Goodnight."

Damien watched her as she approached the footman and greeted him before beginning her walk home. He waited until he wouldn't be noticed before he began to follow, staying in the shadows so that she wasn't aware he was keeping such close attention upon her. He had no idea what her reaction would be to his unsolicited protection, but he could no more bring himself to leave her to walk home through the dark of night than he could decline any of her invitations.

They hadn't gone far, Grace ahead and him trailing a decent distance behind, when suddenly there was an "oomph" from ahead and the footman abruptly went flying to the side. Grace whirled around in sudden alert before she was pushed up against the wall behind her.

Damien had to fight the rush that raced through him, urging him to run over and beat the bloody man senseless, but he had been in enough altercations in his life that rational thought crept in, reminding him that sometimes the best course of action was to keep his position hidden and take advantage of the surprise.

"Hand over your reticule and all your valuables," he heard, and from his position just in the shadows beyond, Damien waited to hear Grace's cry of alarm or fear. Instead, he only heard her calm, reasonable voice.

"If you release me a fraction, I can much better find what you need," she said as though she was speaking to an acquaintance. "I can hardly think with your hands on me like this."

Rage began to course through Damien's veins at the thought of the man touching her as he was, but he needed a moment to determine if the man was acting alone. From the disappearance of the footman, he guessed there were at least two of them.

"Fine, but I've a knife prepared to go into that pretty little throat of yours," came the reply, and Damien balled his fists into his side. At least now he had more information as to what he would be up against.

He heard the rustling of Grace's skirts as she was obviously looking for her reticule. He looked out to see that the thief was similarly interested in what she was doing, and he took advantage of the opportunity.

Damien leaped out of the shadows, tackling the man to the ground, ensuring the knife went flying from his hand. In nearly the same motion, he whirled around behind him, already prepared for the second man to come after him.

He wasn't to be disappointed. Before the attacker could even close in, Damien had slipped a knife out of his boot and thrown it at him, lodging it into his shoulder deep enough for him to howl in pain. Damien grimly smirked in satisfaction before turning around to the first man, hitting him hard enough square in the face for his head to connect with the pavement below him, ensuring that he wouldn't be bothering them — or anyone else — for a good while.

Damien advanced on the other man, collecting his blade after he had finally succeeded in dislodging it.

"Never — and I repeat, *never* — accost innocent women again, do you hear me? Most *especially* this one. If I ever catch you again, you will wish you had never entered this alley."

The man nodded before nearly tripping over himself to reach his friend. He roused him enough to somewhat stand and used his good side to half-drag him out of the street and away from Damien.

That sorted, Damien turned and rushed over to Grace, who was still leaning against the wall, her eyes wide as she stared at him, unmoving, not saying a word.

"Are you hurt?" Damien asked, wrapping his hands around her upper arms as he looked her over, panicked that something had happened he hadn't effectively prevented.

"What did he do? Did he touch you? Did he scare you? Did he..." He couldn't say it aloud.

"I'm fine," she finally said. "I'm fine." Her eyes, however, were darting back and forth, and Damien had the feeling that before long she would realize she wasn't as fine as she thought she was. "Check on William, will you?"

Damien nodded, although he tried to assess her injuries one more time before stepping away to see to the footman, who was already sitting up after his tumble into a doorway. He assured Damien all was well, and after Damien had helped him to his feet, they all continued on their way. This time, Grace didn't bother protesting that she didn't need his escort.

They didn't say much for the next few minutes as they walked the quiet streets of London's Holborn neighbourhood, although Damien was on alert to make sure that no one else would bother them. Once was enough for the evening.

When they finally made it to the narrow grey brick townhouse, Grace told William that she would be in shortly. He looked somewhat wary but hurried inside, likely to tell her father what had happened and who Grace was now with. It didn't give Damien much time.

He stepped toward her, gently taking her hands in his and pulling her into a more secluded area around a plane tree.

"Are you sure you are fine?" Damien asked gently. "I know sometimes after an attack like that it can take some time to come to terms with it."

"I suppose I can admit that the entire episode was much more... violent than I am used to," Grace said slowly before looking up at him, and it took Damien a moment to determine whether he was seeing things in the trick of the dim light, or if those were tears floating within her eyes. "But as hard as it was watching you like that... I think I understand a bit better now. You do what you have to in order to protect others… the people you care about."

Damien nodded slowly, warmth blooming in his heart. He lifted a hand and caressed her cheek, grateful when she didn't pull away.

"I more than care about you, Grace," he said softly, "and I will do anything to look after you properly."

She blinked rapidly as she lifted her face up to his, and Damien couldn't hold back any longer. He lowered his head, placing his lips against hers — gently, at first, giving her a chance to pull away if she chose to.

She didn't.

Instead, she wrapped her arms around his neck and kissed him back with passion he would never have guessed that she felt; she must have kept it locked deep within. Her body melted against him, and he nearly groaned at how perfect it felt to lose himself in her, to give her all of him that had been waiting for her — at first he thought since the moment he had met her, but now he realized it went back further than that. He had been waiting for her his entire life, he just hadn't known it.

He tentatively traced the seam of her lips with his tongue, pleased, relieved, and grateful when she opened to him, inviting him in — an invitation he took full advantage of, furthering his exploration, astonished when he found she reacted to him with the same sense of urgency he was feeling.

Here he had believed that he was the one who was so affected he could barely think straight. Perhaps she had just hidden it much better than he had.

Damien spanned his hands around her hips, pulling her in closer toward him, and her arms tightened around his neck in response. He could have stood there all night, discovering more about her with just this touch, this kiss, until light spilled out onto the walkway beside them, and they sprang apart at the sound and sight.

Damien didn't realize just how much he would miss the sudden loss of her. But as it was her father standing in the doorway, he didn't have much choice.

CHAPTER 13

They stared at each other for a moment, breathing heavily as Grace brought a hand to cover her lips. Had that just happened? Had Damien just kissed her — *passionately* — a kiss that she had *returned*? Those same hands that had just stabbed a man and knocked out another with one punch were those that had pulled her closer, holding her hips still, against him, where she could feel— oh goodness!

"Grace?" Her father's voice boomed out into the night. "Grace, where are you? William just told me—"

"I'm here, Father," she said, stepping out into the light. "And I'm fine."

"Grace," her father said, his tone upon her name a sigh of relief as he practically stumbled down the steps toward her, engulfing her in a very rare embrace. Grace knew he loved all his children, of course, but she didn't realize just how affected he would be at the threat of danger.

"Father, I'm fine. I was actually protected by—"

"By me."

Damien stepped out into the light, his shadow alone

casting such a strong presence that it was difficult for Grace to hide how much he affected her all over again.

"Hondros," her father said, his words tinged with a hint of suspicion. "William told me about your timely appearance."

Damien nodded and Grace suddenly realized that he must have been following her home. At first she was tempted to be insulted, until she realized that if he hadn't, she could now be facing much different circumstances.

"I saw Grace at the lecture and felt it prudent to follow her home — just in case," he said, before cocking his head to the side as one corner of his lips turned up in a slight smile. "I worry."

"Well," her father said, assessing Damien up and down for a moment. "I suppose it is a good thing that you did so, son." He walked over to him and held out his hand. "Thank you."

Damien's eyebrows shot up in surprise, but he recovered quickly and nodded his head as he firmly shook her father's hand. Grace watched them both with interest, realizing that something had changed upon her rescue by Damien.

"Why don't you come in?" her father asked, and when Damien started to protest, he held up a hand. "I insist. I've already opened one of my best bottles of brandy to calm my nerves and since Jeremiah is out, I could use someone to drink it with."

"Of course," Damien said, stepping forward, placing a hand on Grace's back as they walked up the stairs side-by-side. When they reached the top, he abruptly pulled his hand away, but when Grace turned to him, he didn't meet her eyes, instead clasping his hands behind his back and looking down at her. She followed his gaze, her eyes widening when she saw that her dress, over her hips, had a few specks of blood on it, likely from Damien's hands.

She took a breath, her body restless, like she didn't think she should stop moving, that there was this energy within her she needed to get out. That this kiss had just been the beginning, that there was so much more she wanted, needed, from both him and from herself. He had saved her. Perhaps from merely losing her reticule, but it was hard to be certain. She had walked that path many a time before, but why had tonight, the night he had accompanied her, been different?

The first time she had seen him fight, she had been frightened by the violence, repelled by it, if she was being honest. And yet… she was beginning to understand. Could anyone else possibly ever keep her as safe as he had?

The moment before he had kissed her, she had seen, deep within his eyes, the wanting, the yearning, so strong she had been taken aback by it. All of that — for her? She didn't know what she had done to evoke such emotion from within him, and she wasn't entirely sure what to do with it.

But now, when her father was standing there, inviting Damien inside for who knew what kind of inquisition, was not the time to further consider it. That would have to come later.

"Gracie, you're all right?" She glanced up to find that her father was looking on with concern. Thank goodness her mother always went to bed early, for she would be beside herself if she had known that anything was amiss. If only William could have kept the story to himself, but all of her father's employees were far too loyal. Which she supposed was actually a good thing.

"I'm fine, Father, thank you," she said before turning to Damien as she realized she was being dismissed. "Thank you, Mr. Hondros. And goodnight."

"Goodnight Miss Mulberry," he murmured, stealing one last glance before her father led him into the study, closing the door behind him.

* * *

DESPITE MULBERRY'S sudden change in tone, Damien was still wary as he walked into the study and accepted the drink. He took a sip, his eyebrows rising. Mulberry hadn't been wrong — this *was* the best brandy he had ever tasted. He remembered Arie's description of Mulberry's true nature of operations, and wondered where exactly it had come from.

"Exceptional," was all he said, not wanting to give Mulberry any hint that he was aware of where it could have originated.

Mulberry nodded, waving to the large green chairs in front of his desk, so ornate that Damien was sure they must be imported and expensive.

"Take a seat."

Damien dutifully sat as Mulberry took his chair across from him, silent as he gazed at Damien thoughtfully.

"So you're interested in my Gracie."

"I am, sir," Damien said, suddenly reduced to a young man seeking permission. It was not a role he had ever found himself in before.

"Why?"

"Why?" Damien repeated, astonished at the question. "What do you mean?"

"Why her?" Mulberry said, waving his arm. "What is about her that would cause such sudden interest? She's fine enough looking, I suppose, much like her mother, but she isn't exactly striking."

He waited, and Damien tried to determine whether this was a test, or if Mulberry was truly curious as to his interest.

"Well," he began slowly, "she is more intelligent than most *people* I know, let alone women."

Mulberry narrowed his eyes but nodded at Damien to continue.

"She cares about others — puts them first. Is sensitive to what people are thinking and feeling. Is thoughtful about what she says, seeks knowledge and information. She is direct and doesn't hide behind any artifice. Her imagination is limitless and despite her practicality I sense that she has a streak of romanticism in her as well."

Mulberry nodded thoughtfully, stroking his chin.

"That is a lot to determine from a short time of her acquaintance."

"I am a quick study."

"So it seems."

Damien took a sip of his drink, waiting for Mulberry to get to his point. He knew men like Mulberry, and they always had a purpose they were driving at. Most of the time, Damien could ascertain just what that was. But not tonight. Not with this change in Mulberry's attitude.

Mulberry tapped his glass with his index finger.

"I was thinking on the conversation around the dinner table the other night."

Damien waited.

"You mentioned that your brother has a... wide variety of business interests, and that you help him in many aspects of those interests."

"I do," Damien said, revealing nothing about what exactly those were.

"I am beginning to think that we might be able to help one another, as there are certain needs that I am looking to have fulfilled here in London."

Mulberry stood now, walking up and down in front of the fireplace, which blazed cheerily, mocking the wariness between the two men within the room.

"I am going to be taking the family down to Dover for a time in the next couple of weeks. It is getting too hot in London, and Max tells me there are items that need my attention at the docks there. Perhaps you might come with us?"

He stopped walking, turning to Damien.

"Come with you?" Damien repeated, although he didn't give away his surprise. It was not at all what he expected, but it was certainly a welcome invitation, one that both he and Arie would be pleased about, although for entirely different reasons.

"Yes," Mulberry repeated. "You can learn more of our operations, and it will also give you the chance to see if you and Grace might suit. What do you say?"

Damien rubbed his chin, wondering at Mulberry's sudden attitude change toward him but unable to resist the thought of more time with Grace. "I would have to check and make sure I can rearrange a fight, I think, depending on the length of time we are away," he mused, "but I think I could make it work."

"Splendid!" Mulberry said, clapping his hands together, an altogether different man now that he had apparently accepted Damien as a man to be trusted. "I'm sure Grace and my wife will be equally pleased."

Damien certainly hoped so.

He finished his brandy before placing it on the table in front of them. "I shall see you again soon, then, sir."

"So you shall," Mulberry said, walking him to the door, clapping a hand on his shoulder as he did so. "Thank you again for saving my daughter. I mean that with the utmost sincerity."

"Of course, Mulberry," Damien said. "Of course."

* * *

"THIS COULD NOT BE any more perfect," Arie said, rubbing his hands together as he sat across from Damien at the breakfast table the next morning. "You will have access to everything

— and to the side of operations that we need to see. Dover is their smuggling base, Damien, I'm sure of it."

Damien frowned at him as he took a bite of bread.

"I'm not sure I understand why it matters so much that we learn more about it. Isn't the point to gain their trust and then work *with* them?"

"Of course," Arie said smoothly, although Damien didn't miss the glance Diana sent his way and he wondered just what he was missing. "Which we will. But I always like to get more of an understanding about who I am working with before I determine whether it will be the right fit."

"Why don't you just meet with Mulberry? He seems to hold us in higher standing than he did before."

"Which I commend you for, Damien. Good work on following the girl. Did you hire the men to attack her?"

"Did I what?" Damien's fork fell to his plate with a clatter as he stared at Arie sitting across from him. "Of course I didn't. I would never let any potential harm come to Grace." He paused as dread began to grow in his stomach. "You didn't have anything to do with that, did you?"

"Of course not." Arie snorted. "How would I have known that you would be with her at some ridiculous lecture?"

"How do you know anything?" Damien retorted. "Between the two of you, you seem to know what half of London is up to."

Diana looked at him somewhat reproachfully. "That's not fair, Damien. I only gather information that pertains to our business."

"Which is any business or person with two coins to rub together."

Diana ignored him, as she always did anyone she decided was no longer worth arguing with. It had always gotten on Damien's nerves, and not for the first time did he wish that Xander and Calli were still here. They provided a much better balance to the household. Xander was never too far away, but still…

"I will go to Dover, but I am going with the intention of learning more about Grace. I enjoy her company. If her father would like to speak to me on business matters, I will do so, but in the end, Arie, I will suggest that he work with you."

"Very well," Arie said with a shrug, but then his eyes turned hard, cold, and calculating. "Just don't let the girl blind you to who her family truly is. She might be using you just as you are using her."

"Well, *I* am not using her in the slightest," Damien said. "Get that through your thick head."

Silence poured over the table like a bucket of water at that remark. They could tease Arie, sure, but no one ever insulted him. Not even his own brother.

Arie stared at him silently, his expression speaking volumes.

"Enough of this," he said, standing abruptly. "I think we are understood. You will go to Dover. You will bring back the information we need. And if you need to use your relationship with the girl to get it, so be it. Understood?"

Damien didn't respond. He simply picked up his plate and walked out. For there was nothing more to say.

CHAPTER 14

Grace lifted the curtain to peek out the carriage window one more time, just to convince herself that Damien was still there.

She had been shocked when her father had shared the information that Damien was going to accompany them to Dover. She had tried to ask him why he had invited him, but her father, as always, didn't see any reason as to why he should provide her with an answer.

Damien had sent round a note, asking her if she minded that he come. Grace wasn't exactly sure how to say in her response that she didn't mind at all — which was entirely the problem. For instead, she was looking forward to spending more time with him, even if it meant that it would be along with the rest of her family, and she had seen the results of that firsthand.

She had debated inviting Lydia, but had eventually decided that if she couldn't handle her own family, then she was in more trouble than she could ever imagine. Besides, if she invited Lydia, then Damien would be more likely to be left alone with her father and brothers, which she wasn't sure she wanted.

"Not to worry, Grace, he's still there," her mother said with a wide grin as Grace slammed her back against the squabs.

"I was actually trying to determine if I could see the castle in the distance," Grace protested, but her mother just made one of those clucking sounds mothers make that told her she wasn't fooled.

"Has Father changed his mind about Damien, then?" Grace asked, no longer hiding her interest. It seemed her mother was well aware of how she was feeling, no matter how well Grace thought she hid it.

"It seems I have brought him around," her mother said with a wide smile on her face, reminding Grace that her mother had no knowledge of the attack and Damien's rescue — if she did, she would never allow Grace to leave the house again. She reached over and patted Grace's knee. "He is a good man, and I will do anything to see you happy."

To see her *wed*, Grace corrected silently, but she appreciated the support anyway.

"Thank you, Mother."

When they finally reached Dover, Grace took a deep breath of the fresh sea air, happy, as always, to be at the home of their Dover operations, where Max had now taken up residence. From her limited time so far with her father's accounts, she had been surprised to see so little activity from the ports here. From the amount of time her father spent here, as well as Max's involvement and the number of men she had assumed work for her father in Dover, she had always had the perception that most of the shipping came into the port and was then transferred to London.

Perhaps her father was right and her knowledge was rather limited after all.

Instead of the footman helping her down from the carriage, it was Damien who held out a hand to assist her, having already dismounted. She took his offer tentatively, his touch reminding her of the last time she had seen him – which was only a week ago and yet felt like a lifetime. How peculiar. She met his eye, wondering if it was possible that he felt anything akin to the odd notions somehow running through her entire body, even as she told herself to stop being so ridiculous – he was a man, a fighter, not a lovesick romantic.

As soon as they entered the house, however, that was the last she saw of him for a few hours as he was shown to his room and Grace reacquainted herself with her own surroundings. The house was modest, but of course her father ensured that much of his wealth was still on display for anyone who might be visiting, with statues and paintings and other items he had accumulated for his own collections over the years ready to greet his guests.

They took their late dinner in their rooms that night after their day of travel, and Grace quickly fell into bed. She didn't see anyone the next morning and returned to her room to ensure all was in order, but she quickly tired of the four walls of her bedroom and wandered down, out of the house and onto the stretch of grass in front of it. In the distance, she could see the white peaks stretching out across the bay, her own home secluded upon an opposite cliff. There was a path that wound down around the side of the sharp incline, but it was narrow and rocky, although many times as a child she had followed her brothers down it, arriving on the beach below to surprise them, much to her delight and their chagrin.

She was so caught up in her reveries that she jumped at the light touch on her arm, turning in surprise to find Damien behind her.

"You're rather stealthy for a man your size," she said wryly, causing him to laugh.

"So I've been told."

"How do you find the house?" she asked, unsure of what else to say, before returning her gaze to the horizon. The image of him here, in front of her, at her home away from home was nearly too much, for it seemed so perfect, so right, but she wasn't sure if she was yet ready to imagine a future that featured him so permanently within it.

"It's impressive," he said with a smile, and she nodded.

"So my mother and father would like everyone to feel."

"This view, though," he heaved out a breath, "it is something else."

"Nothing like this in London," she said with a smile, tilting her head toward him.

"That is for certain."

"Have you been outside of London much before?" she couldn't help but ask, though she wondered if she was overstepping.

"Not since I was young — too young to remember anything else," he said, and she longed to ask more, but a faraway look had entered his eyes, so she refrained. "And you?"

"Mostly just here," she said. "Father has always been so involved with his work that there never seems to be the opportunity to go anywhere else, as much as Mother begs him to take her travelling. But I have no complaints. I travel enough through the stories I read."

Her cheeks immediately warmed as she realized how providential she must sound, but when he nodded knowingly, she was somewhat relieved.

"There is that. Did you spend much of your childhood here?"

"I did when I was a bit older — I believe my father bought

this house around the time I turned ten and we spent many summers here." She smiled as the memories returned. "There's the path to the shore, right beside that oak tree. I was just thinking about the times I followed my brothers down it to the shore, and how fortunate I was that my mother never discovered what I was up to. We spent so much of our time exploring the caves."

"There are caves below?" he asked with interest, and she nodded.

"They are huge and stretch back farther than one would ever think."

"Are they used for anything?"

"They weren't when I was young," she said, then lifted a hand. "As for now, I couldn't say. I haven't been down in ages."

"We will have to go exploring."

"We will."

"I would actually suggest we go now — it's been so long since I've been near the water — but the tides would not be on our side and we could find ourselves trapped."

"A shame."

"It is, actually," she said, surprised by how much she meant it. "Would you like to do some exploring of another kind?"

"What did you have in mind?" he asked, his eyes darkening somewhat, and Grace swallowed hard as she realized how her words could be misconstrued.

"I, ah, only meant that perhaps I could show you around the grounds here, take you to town and to see the base of my father's operations, if you'd like."

Her father's operations? Why was she reminding him that there was another reason to be here, a reason besides her?

"I would like that," he said softly.

Grace led him around the side of the house before they

took to the much more well-formed path they had travelled upon arrival. The town spread out before them, the carefully preserved historic structures dotting the landscape.

"It's beautiful in its own way, isn't it?" Grace asked, looking up at him with a smile. "I think I would rather like to live somewhere such as this."

"Would you now?"

She nodded. "Although there is much to be said for London. Their bookshops and libraries, for example, are far superior, although the local bookseller will bring in anything I ask of him."

"Rather generous of him."

"It is. Especially as we don't spend much time here."

Grace was pleased to find that she encountered many familiar faces, and that they recognized her in turn, even though she hadn't visited since the previous summer. She could sense Damien watching her with interest, and she wasn't entirely sure just how to introduce him to the people they met. She settled for a 'guest of her family's', as it was the truth.

Finally they rounded the corner of Townwall Street to the harbour, and she led him down to the end, where three of her father's ships sat, waiting to be either unloaded or for more goods to be added to them.

"I recall his fleet being much larger here," she said as they stood on the dock, "however most are out at sea, of course. Come, I'll show you where he stores all the goods."

She opened the door of the closest warehouse, leading Damien within, and was pleased when her eldest brother was the one to greet them.

"Gracie!" he said with outstretched arms. "I didn't realize you would come today. I left early before anyone awoke to try to get my work done early, before Father joined me. I see you've brought company." He nodded a greeting toward Damien, his voice becoming more guarded. "Hondros."

"Mulberry," Damien responded. "Good to see you again."

Grace had to roll her eyes at the bravado the two men exuded, even though they were not rivals at all, but two men who were protective of her for entirely different reasons. She would have to make it clear to Max that Damien was not a man he had to be wary of.

"Did Father ask the two of you to come?" Max said, eyeing both of them curiously, and Grace shook her head.

"No, he actually doesn't know that we're here. We explored on our own volition."

"He said something about bringing Hondros around once you arrived, which is why I ask," Max said. "But since you're here, I'll show you where business is done."

He led them around, showing them the offices, the stores of material that had been shipped in, where it was all loaded onto wagons to be shipped to London, and finally back out to the docks.

"And that's it," he said, lifting his arms.

"It is?" Grace frowned. "I could have sworn—"

"That's it, Gracie," Max said, an edge of warning to his tone that she did not appreciate but she wasn't about to question in front of Damien. He must have sensed it as well, for he took a slight step forward, and Grace quickly tried to diffuse the tension in the air.

"Very well. See you at dinner?" Grace asked, to which Max agreed before she and Damien took their leave, beginning back up the hill toward the heart of town once more.

Grace found herself huffing slightly at the incline, frowning at Damien when he showed no sign that he was putting out any effort whatsoever.

"My family seems rather intent on involving you in their business interests," she said, reaching up and tugging at the strings of her bonnet, for they were beginning to drive her mad with their itching. "Why would that be? What is it, exactly, that your family does besides own a gaming hell?"

Damien subjected her to an assessing gaze, as though trying to determine just whether or not he should tell her the truth. Grace desperately wished he would, but in the same breath, she would never force him to. If he chose not to trust her, then she would have to decide what to do from there.

"My family," he said slowly, cautiously, looking away before returning his face to meet her gaze, "are thieves."

CHAPTER 15

Grace let out a sound that was half-laugh, half-snort as she stopped mid-stride, staring at him incredulously.

"Thieves. Your family are thieves."

"Yes," he said, unsure exactly what to make of her reaction. Was she trying to deny the truth or did she truly think he was jesting?

He realized the latter as she laughed again. "That's preposterous!"

"I wish it was," he said, lifting his hands slowly, "but it's the truth."

"You own a gaming hell," she said, her smile falling as she obviously realized just how serious he was.

"We do," Damien confirmed. "We have a few legitimate business connections as well."

Much like your own father, he longed to say, but now was not the time to turn everything back around on her family. The truth, however, was that the two families were very much alike. Only, Grace had been kept in the dark her entire life. Damien hadn't been sure how she would respond, but one thing he had been sure of, was that he was not going to lie to her.

"What do you steal?" she asked, continuing to walk once more, her stride faster, her expression, from what he could see, somewhat troubled.

"It depends," Damien said slowly. "My brother, Arie, usually organizes somewhat elaborate schemes to steal from those who won't miss it. Most of us — my brothers and sisters, that is — began as pickpockets of one sort or another, but we do nothing like that anymore. We plan ruses such as… stealing a painting from a duke who wouldn't miss it, or jewels from a rich, crooked baron."

Grace turned to him now, and Damien was pleased that she had, at least, removed her bonnet so that he could better see her, that she couldn't completely hide from him.

"What role do you play in all of this?"

"It depends," he said. "The role of protector, sometimes, of another set of eyes, or if strength is needed to move something — or someone — I take on that role."

"I see," Grace said. "And you fight."

"I do," Damien confirmed, already growing increasingly nervous that the more they spoke of this, the less she would want to do with him. "Arie believes that if my… strength is shown in public, it will make others less likely to try to interfere with our family."

Grace said nothing for a few strides as they walked through town before turning up the hill toward her family's home, and Damien didn't push her, as desperate as he was to know what she was thinking.

When they began up the walk toward her family's narrow, red-brick townhouse, she stopped, turning to him, her eyes wide and voluminous. "Thank you for telling me," she said. "I appreciate the truth."

"Of course," he said.

"But you never answered my question."

"Which was?"

"Why does my family want you to know so much about their operations if you are from a family that could potentially… take from them?"

"Grace," Damien said, stepping toward her and placing his hands gently around her upper arms, "I would never steal from you. Or your family."

"I believe you," she said, her words just above a whisper, warming Damien through. For right now, that was all that mattered.

"I best get prepared for dinner," she said. "I shall see you then?"

"Of course," Damien said, "I look forward to it."

The rest of the evening progressed rather smoothly, and it seemed to Damien that, as Grace guessed, he was being accepted into the family's fold. He assumed that if he didn't arouse any suspicions, Grace's father could very well be open to discussions about a partnership.

But first, Damien had a few questions of his own — questions that, perhaps, Arie wouldn't overly care about, but Damien did. He had to know all that Mulberry was smuggling into England. While he knew that the goods included spirits, cigars, and clothing material from France, he had to be sure that Mulberry wasn't involved in anything that would include trading in… less scrupulous items. Damien may not have a great deal of morals, but there were some that he refused to break, no matter the circumstance.

He woke the next morning just as the sun was beginning to creep over the horizon, pushing himself out of bed and dressing hurriedly. His plan was to find his way to the caves below before anyone else awoke. By his estimate, if he timed everything right, he should be able to descend the cliff slope, sneak into the caves and take a quick look around, then return before the tide and Grace came to find him.

The morning air was brisk but refreshing as he stayed as close to the house as possible before looking for the tree Grace had pointed out the day before. He felt somewhat guilty at using her information in what she might see as a form of deception, but he didn't know what other solution he could attempt. For he had already decided that it was up to her family to reveal their own misdeeds and secret activity to her.

The only ones he would share were his own, which she could take or leave. He had no idea how to actually get through, to uncover what was beneath that shell of hers, but he had the feeling that he was getting closer and closer to breaking in.

Damien found the path easily, but quickly realized that Grace had been right — it was a narrow trail, and a rather slippery one too, filled with sliding rocks and branches that reached out to scratch at him. He assumed that there must be another way through the caves, for there was no possibility that goods could be transported up this slippery, steep path.

When he reached the bottom, he was surprised to find that his feet hit sand. He looked around, trying to determine where these caves might be, but if they were here, they were well-hidden. He ran his hand along the wall of the cliffs as he carefully searched, not wanting to miss anything as he went.

Finally — there. Just up ahead, there was a crack in the cliff wall. Damien lifted the lantern he had brought with him to see within what was sure to be the darkened cave, and took a step forward, anxious at just what he might find.

Grace had always been an early riser.

She just hadn't been aware that Damien was as well.

She had been dressing — she could dress in a simple morning gown without the help of a maid — when she had spied a figure through her window, which overlooked the cliffs beyond.

It couldn't be Damien — could it? Ire grew within Grace that he would attempt such an exploration without her, after she had been the one to show him the path. She thought that this was an adventure they would undertake together — and there he was, going off alone.

She crossed her arms over her chest, telling herself not to worry over it anymore — that if that was his choice, then so be it. But then she remembered the tides. Would he know the signs to watch for? Would he know how high they could get? Usually this early in the morning, just after the sun began to peek over the ocean's horizon, high tide would hit. It was not a problem if one was high enough on the beach, but it could trap someone in the cave below.

Grace shivered as she remembered the one time, as a girl, she had followed her brothers down there. She had remained hidden from them, sure that if they noticed her, they would force her to return to the house.

Instead, she had gotten lost in the maze of the caves beneath the cliffs. The entrance near the mouth of the cave had begun to fill with water, and Grace had been stranded, alone, certain that she was going to meet her end by drowning in the darkness, where no one would ever find her. As it turned out, the water never reached her, but it came close enough to cause her imagination to run rather freely.

The memory was enough to spur her into action, and she threw on a cloak to ward off the chill of the morning before dashing down the stairs and out the garden door off the back parlour toward the cliff, hoping none of the early risers —the few servants — would notice her.

She inhaled deeply at the start of the path, wondering how often it had been used recently. Damn Damien. If only he had waited for her, it would have been much safer for both of them.

Grace looked around, finding a branch that would suffice as a walking stick if she broke off the top of it. Once that was dealt with, she curled her hand around the end to help her down the steep descent. The waves were already crashing onto the sand below, and she had to remind herself to watch where she was going instead of craning her neck in search of Damien's bulky figure.

Once, twice, her foot slipped on rocks that slid out from under her, but she was able to dig her makeshift walking stick into the ground to catch herself. She was still grumbling when she reached the bottom, ready to cuss out Damien for putting her through such a thing alone.

Fortunately for him, he was nowhere to be found, and Grace wondered if he could possibly have found the entrance to the nearest cave without any guidance.

But it was Damien. A man who, apparently, was from a family of thieves. She could still hardly believe that he was telling the truth about that. Was it possible? Or was he simply trying to see how gullible she was? Could he possibly be hiding something else?

What could be worse than being part of such an organization, she had no idea, and she didn't want to allow herself to imagine just what that could be.

She found the entrance herself, taking a look back to try to decide just how much time she had before high tide came in. The sea was gaining, that was for certain, and it was an opponent one could never vanquish.

She would have to find Damien quickly.

She slipped around the corner and into the mouth of the cave, which was larger than it seemed when approaching from the side near her family's house. It was as dark as she had remembered, and she sighed in relief that she had the foresight to pocket the tinderbox before she left her room. The lantern was, as it had always been, hanging from a rocky outcropping upon entering the cave. Her father had put it there after the incident in which she had been stranded — he told her that he would make sure she would never be left alone in the dark again.

Grace had never quite overcome that fear. It was ridiculous, for it was a child's fear, not the fear of a grown woman. She knew, now, just how natural the dark was, and that the only thing to be afraid of was what the darkness hid.

But that was still a valid fear. Especially in a cave that had likely not been explored in some time.

"Damien?" she called as she stepped into the cave, hoping he would be nearby.

No such luck. She drew another long breath, forcing herself to walk in deeper, calling his name, but heard only the echoed response of her own voice as it returned to her.

"Damien?" she called again. "If you are planning to scare me, then I will warn you right now that I will not find it funny."

When still nothing returned to her, she forced herself to round the corner, to where the tunnel began to open up to a larger cavern, where the water from another entrance reached the center. She frowned as she swung the lantern around to take a closer look. If she wasn't mistaken, there were footprints at her feet — and not just her own footprints or possibly Damien's, but many, as though there had been quite a gathering here, and rather recently at that.

But who would even know about these caves? They were directly underneath her family's property, and Max would have no reason to invite anyone down here when he had an entire house and warehouse at his disposal.

Perhaps someone was trespassing on their land — not that they owned the caves nor the beach, but it was difficult to access this by any other way… except through the caves themselves.

She was so wrapped up in her ponderings that she didn't even notice something — or someone — approaching from behind her until it was too late.

When the touch came on her shoulder, she screamed aloud.

CHAPTER 16

"Shh, it's all right. It's just me."

"Damien!" Grace said, allowing him to turn her around to face him, her brown eyes wide in her face when she did. "You scared me. Again."

"Well, you did wander alone into a dark cave," he couldn't help teasing her, to which she swatted him on the shoulder.

"I was only following *you*!"

"Ah, you're following me now, love?" He quirked a brow. "I must be doing something right then."

She narrowed her brows in what he was sure was supposed to be an expression of disapproval. "As it happens, I am something of an early riser. I saw you go down the path and couldn't help but wonder why you would attempt such an exploration alone — without me."

Ah. So that was the source of her ire — she felt that she had been left out of his adventure. He remembered, however, the journey down the cliff face treacherous, even for him, and he frowned at her.

"You shouldn't have walked that path alone."

"I have descended that cliff so many times before. I would

argue that you were the one who decided to forge the path on your own instead of together."

He couldn't argue that, as much as he didn't exactly enjoy the thought of her putting herself in danger — in any regard.

She placed her lantern on the floor before walking in a circle in front of him. "What are you doing down here, anyway?"

"As you said," he responded easily, "exploring."

"By yourself, at the rising of the sun?" she asked. "I find that hard to believe."

"I'm an early riser as well," he said, hating that he was lying to her but only doing so in order to protect her from the truth — the truth of her family's hidden business. He only wished that she had some knowledge of it already, so that they could truly understand one another's motivations.

She eyed him warily but continued her path before looking down below her. "Someone else has been exploring — plenty of someones."

"I see that."

"I'll have to ask Max if he's been down here."

"I doubt your brother has any reason to be," Damien said, not wanting to explain to her family just why he had been down here — and not only that, but down here alone with Grace. "It could be someone who has entered from elsewhere."

"There are many ways to access the cave, although none of them are particularly easy," she mused. "Some become so filled with water that you need to make sure to enter by boat."

Suddenly she gasped, and Damien instinctively grabbed her arm as he looked around to see what could have caused such fright. "What's wrong?"

"Water — the tides," she said quickly, bending to pick up

her lantern before taking his hand with her free one. "We have to go or we could be trapped in here."

Being trapped inside with her didn't actually seem too bad of an idea. As long as they didn't get overcome by sea water, he could think of worse ways to pass the time.

Of course, there were the potential repercussions of what her family would say, but this would be a legitimate excuse, would it not?

He easily kept up with her, his own lantern in hand, as she slowed while reaching each corner.

"This way — I think," she said, her voice no longer curious, teasing, or questioning but rather tremulous, as though something had frightened her.

"Grace," Damien called, tugging at her hand when she didn't look back. "Grace," he repeated, and finally she slowed a step.

"Yes?"

"What is wrong?" he asked, reading the panic in her eyes. "The tides couldn't possibly come high enough to flood this cave — could they? I was watching them yesterday, and figured at most they would lap the entrance."

"They wouldn't flood the cave, no," she said, shaking her head. "But we could be trapped in here. Alone. In the dark. We—"

"Grace," he said, pulling her closer to him. "If that happens, we'll be fine. I promise."

He couldn't understand why, when moments before she had seemed perfectly fine with her adventure into the caves, that she would suddenly be reduced to such sheer anxiety. She didn't seem to have any desire to explain it to him, however, as she turned and continued her mission of finding the entrance.

The only thing he could do now was continue to follow

her, and perhaps he would eventually stumble upon whatever was causing her such issue.

Grace stopped so abruptly that Damien ran right into the back of her, dropping his lantern as he reached out an arm to steady her.

"What's wrong?" he asked, although he quickly saw for himself. They were still fairly far back from the entrance, but already the sea water was beginning to creep up, invading the space, pushing them back farther and farther.

Grace said nothing, but from where she stood in the circle of his arms, he could feel how tense, how on edge she was. Damien tilted his head down toward her, his voice coming right beside her ear.

"Grace," he said softly, "turn around."

When she finally did as he asked, it was slowly, stiltedly, as though she was a wooden doll that he was using strings to command. When she had finished her circle, she looked up at him with wide eyes.

"We're trapped," she said, her voice just above a whisper, to which Damien nodded slowly.

"Somewhat — for now. But the tides will go down, and we will be able to walk out again. With any luck, no one will have yet risen for the day."

"My family is always awake early."

"Then we will explain that we were exploring and were trapped. Problem solved," Damien said with a smile that was supposed to alleviate her fears but didn't seem to have the desired effect. "If you truly feel that you cannot stay here another moment, the water likely isn't deep. We can wade to the foot of the cliffs."

"I can't swim," she said, biting her lip.

"Nor can I," Damien said with a shrug. "But I'm sure we'll be fine."

Grace rapidly shook her head, and Damien was pleased to

see that, with their small argument, at least some life was returning to her countenance. "That's too great a chance to take — for both of us. You may know everything one might need in London, Damien, but here, I am much more versed in the nature of the sea and land above us."

"On that, I'm sure you are right."

"I'm always right."

Their exchange coaxed a small grin from her, which Damien returned. "You see? All will be fine."

Their boots, however, were beginning to dampen, and he tried to lead her deeper into the cave without her noticing.

She caught onto his sleeve anyway, her fingers tightening around him.

"Your lantern is out."

"But yours is still lit," he countered. "And from where we are standing, some of the natural light is filtering in."

He looked around him, finding that if they retreated a few paces, where the cave narrowed there was a rocky outcropping.

"Come here," he said, leading her over to it, taking the lantern from her and setting it down beside them as they sat down next to one another, their thighs pressing together due to the small space they occupied. "Tell me, Grace, what's wrong?"

He wanted to know everything that frightened her, wanted to know what was bothering her, so that he could fix it for her, smooth away her problems and make everything better.

Her eyes were fixed somewhere on the wall across from her, but at least her words told him some of what he needed to know.

"It's the dark. The small space. Getting trapped."

"But that won't happen," he protested. "And I'm here with you."

"Once... when I was young, I was trapped in here," she said, her words so quiet that he almost missed them. "It took me hours to find my way out, and my family had no idea I was down here. I had followed my brothers but never let them see me. When I finally found the entrance, it was high tide, full of water as it is right now, and I was so petrified by fear I could barely move."

Understanding dawned as she spoke. "And you are fearful of that happening again."

"I can't properly explain it," she said, looking down at her hands. "I know it's foolish, that I'm a grown woman now and have no reason to find myself lost in these caves."

"Are they natural caves?"

"No, I don't think so," she said, tilting her head to the side, and Damien sensed that his questions were, at least, getting her out of her own head and anxieties as she considered the answers. "I believe my father told me they were originally dug as people were mining for flint and lime. They moved on, however, when they found nothing here."

"But they are connected in other areas?"

"A few, yes. I cannot say that I spent much time discovering more about them after my... incident within them."

"Understandable."

Damien risked placing his arm around her shoulders, hoping that some contact would help her focus on something besides her fear.

"Tell me, Grace," he said, finding that his voice had become huskier than he would have liked, "are you happy that I'm here with you?"

"Well, I wouldn't be here if it wasn't for you," she said, some spirit in her words, to which Damien laughed.

"That, I understand. But I mean, here, in Dover, with your family. I didn't realize it would feel so... natural."

She glanced up at him, some of the panic gone, to be

replaced by some impishness and… interest. "It does, doesn't it?"

"Have you forgiven me for my violent ways?"

She didn't say anything for a moment, instead looking down at her hands. "The thing is, Damien, the more I come to know about you, the less I believe that you actually *are* violent, in any way."

"How can you say that?" He frowned. "You have seen what I can do on more than one occasion."

"That is true, yes," she acknowledged. "But I don't think that is who you are. Not really. When it comes down to it, you actually seem to be much more of a peacemaker than anything else."

Damien's eyes widened in surprise that she had stumbled upon the truth. It was a running joke within his family, that despite the fact he was the one who used his fists to solve problems, when it came to those he loved, he only wanted to see them in harmony with one another.

"You are perceptive," he acknowledged.

"I don't have much else to occupy my time with," she said somewhat self-deprecatingly.

"Grace," he said, stretching out the syllable of her name.

"Damien," she said, teasingly mocking him.

"Take a compliment."

"Fine. Thank you," she said with a bit of a shiver.

"Are you cold?" Damien asked. He had always been warmer than the average person, and with his heavy cloak, hadn't even noticed that the high tide brought with it a chill that ran through the cave.

"A little," she said. "But I'll be fine. It shouldn't be much longer now."

Damien stood, lifting her to her feet. He unclasped his cloak, holding it toward her.

"Here, put this on."

"Oh no, I couldn't," she protested, but he only stepped closer to her, lightly batting her hands away.

"I insist," he said, reaching around her to settle it upon her. The moment he did so, however, it brought the two of them closer together, until they were standing face to face, just inches from one another.

"Better?" he murmured, beginning to fasten it under her chin, and he knew he should step back, move away, but he couldn't bring himself to do so any more than he couldn't stop himself from following her to Dover, even when he knew that he might only be making things harder for the two of them if it wasn't going to work out in the long run.

"Better," she said, her voice hitching as her throat worked, as affected as he was.

The cloak fastened, he trailed his fingers up her cheek, threading them into her hair, which was still quite loose as she obviously hadn't had any attention from her lady's maid that early in the morning.

Damien was glad of it. He wanted to see what her hair looked like cascading down around her shoulders, and he succumbed to the urging within him to release it from its few pins, until her dark blond hair surrounded her shoulders, waving around her face. It softened her features, causing his desire for her to grow even stronger, to the point that she would have to push him away if she wanted to keep him from kissing her.

"Grace," he nearly whispered, the puff of his breath pushing away strands of hair from beside her temple, his word a silent question, a supplication for her to allow him to kiss her. She nodded her acceptance, her willingness, and she tilted her head up toward him, an invitation that he could never refuse.

Their lips met, for just a couple of breaths, in what could be described as a silent, moving hesitancy as they asked and answered their questions of one another — whether this was what they each wanted, and how far they would go, whether Grace would welcome the distraction from her fears or whether she was too preoccupied to have any thought of what was happening between the two of them.

But all of Damien's concerns were alleviated by the pressure of her mouth, the insistence of her arms wrapping around his neck, as they drew him down, closer to her, the way her body pressed into his and made him forget nearly everything else about their circumstance or the various reasons as to why he was in Dover.

For only one thing mattered — right now, and every other moment that came before and after it. Grace. Most of the women who were drawn to Damien were those who were rather straightforward, who had no qualms about practically throwing themselves at him after he fought, so overcome were they by his physical prowess.

But Grace was different. Grace saw aspects of him that no one else ever had. She understood what motivated him, she saw through everything he presented to the world to discover the man he was underneath.

And somehow, for some reason, she accepted all of the parts of him that were rather unsavoury. He had no idea why, but he was forever grateful.

His hands slid from her hair, beneath her cloaks and along her back to cup her hips, holding her firmly against him. He was sure she could feel how much he wanted her as his arousal must be pressing into her belly, but she made no effort to pull away, which only furthered his desire. The thin material of her dress did little to hide her figure, and he wished he could lose himself in the lushness of her curves. He took a step forward, pressing her against the wall behind them, one hand wrapping around her back to make sure that she was protected from the rough stone of the cave.

The water that had been so threatening to her earlier now provided a peaceful backdrop that reminded him that they were alone, that no one would be interrupting them or startling them out of this embrace that had encompassed them both. Whoever had been present in these caves, at whatever point in time, was long gone. While her entire family might be living and slumbering far above them through the centuries-old rock, it seemed this cave had been built for this very purpose, to provide them this chance to be alone and focused only on each other.

Grace broke away from him for but a moment, murmuring against his lips, so softly that he didn't hear her the first time. Her breathing was as rough as his, the two of them intermingled, so that he hardly knew where he ended and she began.

"What was that?"

"I just said I am much warmer now," she said, looking up at him, her eyes hazy with desire. "I think you can have your cloak back."

He unclasped it but made no effort to put it back on, instead letting it slide to the floor.

"I've no need of it."

"Or perhaps you do."

He lifted an eyebrow, unsure of what she meant by that.

"Why don't you lay it out on the ground?"

"For what?" he said, confused, unsure of just what she might be frightened of.

But when she slid her arms around his waist and looked up at him, there was no sign of fear in her eyes. Just longing. When she spoke, her voice was raspy, but sure.

"To make love to me."

CHAPTER 17

Dear Lord, please let him say something, Grace silently prayed as she looked up into Damien's eyes, willing him to say anything at all, but he just stood there, wide-eyed, showing no emotion besides, perhaps... shock?

Did he think her scandalous? Forward? Grace had been as surprised as anyone when the words had come pouring from her mouth. But she was a woman who based most of her decisions on fact and reason, and what she knew right now was that she wanted Damien with a desperation she would never have thought possible had she not felt it with all of her being. She also knew that she had never been pulled like this to a man before and likely never would again. And, from what she could ascertain, he was equally as attracted to her, although why, she couldn't quite understand.

All in all, it led to an opportunity that she might never again have in her entire life. For she wouldn't marry a man just to appease her mother, and whether or not Damien was serious about pursuing this courtship into something more than it currently was, she had no idea, but all she could control was this moment in time.

If Damien was of the same mind.

"I—" he finally choked out. "Grace, I—we— That is to say, I'm not sure—"

She held up a hand, mortified. He didn't want her — not in the way she thought. And now she had put him in this position where he had to deny her, but likely felt terrible for doing so, especially after she had acted so foolishly scared for no reason at all. He had probably only been trying to distract her, and she had taken it much too far.

"It's fine, honestly. You can say no. Of course. Of course you can say no. I should never have suggested it. I just thought… well, I thought there would never be another opportunity like this. And that I want to, and I thought you wanted to, but if you don't, then no harm done."

She attempted a smile, but could feel it wobble on her lips, and she could only hope that he wouldn't know how much it hurt to be turned down like this, even when he was being ever the gentleman.

"Grace…" He stopped her, his hands wrapping around her upper arms as gently as could be. "Of *course* I want to. I want this — *you* — more than I've ever wanted anything in my entire life. But I don't want to do anything that you might regret later. This is not to be taken lightly."

"Do you?" she asked, eyeing him shrewdly. "That is to say, have you ever taken *this* lightly before?"

"Well… yes," he said, though he looked somewhat ill at the confession.

"Then what difference does it make now?"

"The difference is you," he said, his eyes boring into hers in earnest. "You matter. More than any other woman ever has before."

"If I matter so much," she said, setting her chin in determination, "then please, respect that I can make a decision of importance just as much as you can. That this is what I want.

That you have proven yourself to be the man that I always thought you were, and allow me to choose *you*."

He didn't say anything for what felt like an eternity, until finally the consternation fell from beneath his brows, and Grace knew that she had broken through, that he had finally given in to what they both wanted — and needed. Grace was suddenly extremely grateful for all that Lydia had told her about what this desire led to — courtesy of Lydia's older sister.

He threaded his fingers into her hair, a sensation that felt better than anything she had ever felt before — so far.

"Very well," he said, nipping at her bottom lip. "If you insist."

"I do."

He let out a growl more primitive than any sound she had ever heard him make, even when he had been in the middle of the boxing ring, and her breath caught in her throat.

The second cloak soon tumbled to the ground, joining the first, and Damien left her for a moment as he re-arranged them on the cave floor, providing a much softer surface. He didn't seem ready to take her down there, yet, however, as instead he returned to her lips, now that his decision had been made taking them hungrily, desperately, and she returned the passion with equal fervour.

His hands — those strong hands that were capable of such violence yet such surprising gentleness as well, slid around her waist and then up higher, cupping her ribs and finally finding purchase beneath her breasts, teasing them, loving them from every angle until his fingertips found her nipples through the soft fabric of her dress. Grace threw her head back, gasping at the sensations that flowed from his fingers, through nerve endings that she had never known could be so achingly erotic as he shifted his fingers back and forth, causing warmth to pool deep within her at the very place she so longed for him.

"Damien," she gasped, and he leaned her back against the wall, his knee coming between her legs, and she felt so utterly wanton as she couldn't stop herself from rubbing against the thick rigidness of his thigh. Whatever he thought of her now, she had no idea, but it seemed that all her inhibitions had fled and she no longer cared. All that mattered was feeling... *more.* She didn't want him to stop, and could hardly express the unnamed thickness of emotion that filled her, the thrill that overwhelmed her. She had no idea how to put what she was feeling into words, how to tell him what she needed, but it seemed that he already knew, as every time he touched her, it only fueled the longing that was already deep within.

He pushed down the soft muslin of her dress, and Grace was glad that she had thrown on a morning dress that was easy to fasten herself as it meant that it was equally as easy to shrug out of — or for Damien to find his way into.

The rough, calloused skin of his fingers and palms scraped deliciously over the soft expanse of her breasts, and Grace arched herself into him while he continued his onslaught, until he pushed the sleeves off her shoulders. The chill of the sea air tingled against her skin, but Grace wasn't cold — rather she was warmed right through, and she wasn't sure how much more of this she could take. She still, however, had enough wits about her that she couldn't help the immediate response to try to cover herself from his eyes, afraid that he wouldn't be pleased with what he saw — but he surprised her by reaching out and tugging her arms down.

"Don't," he said, his voice rough. "You're beautiful and I want to see more."

Well, two could play that game, she thought then. She pushed off the sleeves of his jacket, eager to see what was hiding underneath. She had felt the firm muscle of his chest before, had seen it from across the room at the boxing ring, but to be able to touch it, this close…

He helped her, sliding the jacket and then his shirt quickly off his body, and Grace sucked in a breath as she stared at him. She lifted a hand nearly reverently, sliding her fingers over the coarse hairs of his chest.

He was magnificent. She had known that, of course, but somehow, up close, having complete access to him with his full desire present was an entirely different experience.

And one that she never wanted to end.

When Grace finally summoned the nerve, she looked up to meet his eye and was both shocked and thrilled to find that he seemed just as affected as she was, his head tilted back, his eyes half-shut, the cords of his neck straining. It filled her with a heady sense of power that she could bring such a man to the edge of his restraint.

She decided to test the limits, inching her fingers lower until they reached the edge of his breeches. She hesitated for but a moment — not long enough for him to do anything about it — before she began to clumsily unfasten the fall of his breeches until it lay open before her.

Grace teased her fingers along the edges, letting them travel ever-so-slowly below until she had to stop with a hard swallow when she reached his shaft, which was now straining toward her.

"Go on," he said, his voice gutted as he began to return in kind, sliding his rough hands along her hips, and she realized that as she had been occupied he had been inching her dress down until it lay just below her hipbones. She would have been embarrassed at standing so bare before him had she not been so overcome by the heady desire coursing through her.

As he seemed to enjoy what she was doing, she summoned all of the courage within her — which had been incredibly bolstered by her desire — and reached below to stroke him. She was shocked by the soft skin that covered him, so at odds with the hard steel of him below.

"My word, Grace," he muttered into her ear, and he let her continue for only a few moments before he abruptly pulled back and away from her, then lifted her feet from under her and spread her back on the cloaks below them.

Grace no longer felt the cold of the cave, the spray of the ocean, nor the hardness of the floor below her. She acknowledged it all in the back of her mind, but it was pushed away by the man before her, who took up all the space her senses would allow.

Damien spread out on top of her, removing her dress completely now, his body enough to keep her warm. Grace had no idea when he had removed his breeches, but they were gone, and all that was left was the two of them with nothing at all between them, nor anything around them but the natural world which had always been here and always would be.

He planted a kiss just below her breasts before returning to place one more earth-shattering kiss on her lips that left her shaking — especially when she could feel him on her thigh, ready and waiting to enter her. She had no idea why he hadn't gotten to it yet, but then he slid a hand down and stroked her right where she ached for him and she realized that there was, apparently, more to it than the main event.

Grace gasped when he slid one finger into her, then another, as his thumb rubbed at her sensitive nub until she was writhing beneath him and a slow burn began deep within her, one that promised to burst if only she could find the end of it.

It was then that Damien slid his fingers out and nudged himself right against her entrance, but stopped short, leaning down toward her and resting his forehead against hers.

"Are you sure?" he asked, his voice strained, the muscles of his shoulders taut.

"More than anything," she replied, her breath coming in hard pants, and with that he slowly began to slide into her.

Grace had no idea what she was doing, but it seemed most natural to lift her legs into the air, wrapping them around him, which was apparently right as he fit into her much more smoothly after that. There was an initial slight burn on his entrance that wasn't entirely painful, but neither did it continue the sensations that had been building under the mastery of his fingers.

When he stopped, however, it allowed her a moment to get used to the feel of him, so deep within her, and when he murmured in her ear, asking if she was all right, she nodded into his shoulder. He began to move, gently and slowly at first, his speed increasing as she became more used to him, until she no longer remembered any unpleasantness as she was so overwhelmed by the intensity of pleasure, and the crest she began to ride. Then he reached down and rubbed against her once more and she crested over the top as the waves ebbed through her in such sweet release that tears began to trickle out of her eyes.

A few more strokes and Damien was withdrawing from her, spending himself on the cave floor beside them, and she missed him for the few seconds he was gone. Quickly, however, he returned to her, drawing her close as he wrapped one of the cloaks around them, keeping her tight against him.

Grace faced him, her nose deep into his chest as she could no longer smell the sea but instead inhaled everything that was uniquely Damien.

He pressed a kiss against her temple as he ran a hand over her hair, and never in her life had Grace ever felt so loved, so treasured — even if it was only for the moment and not for forever.

"Are you all right?" he asked softly in her ear, and she nodded against him.

"Better than all right," she said. "That was… everything."

"I agree," he said with a slight chuckle, and she smiled into him. She had no idea if she would ever experience something like this again — with him, or with anyone else — but she had this now. A memory, at the very least, that she could never lose.

CHAPTER 18

Damien couldn't keep the smile from his face for the rest of the day.

He knew he should never have taken Grace's innocence. If he had, it should have been in the marriage bed, in a place where she could be properly worshipped and cared for afterward.

Yet somehow, there in that cave, in that moment, it had seemed perfect in a way that he couldn't properly explain. When she had asked him, he had found that he didn't have the power within him to say no.

As for now… well, he could only see one way forward from here. He had to ask Grace to marry him.

The thought actually filled him with a heady sense of excitement rather than dread, as he had always thought marriage would. Xander had told him recently that when the right woman came along, it would change all of his notions about marriage. Xander had been right. For he couldn't imagine anything better than every day with Grace.

Yes, there was much they would have to determine. He knew that Grace only hesitantly accepted his past and his life rather than wholeheartedly approved. And yet he didn't feel quite as guilty about bringing her into his life as he might otherwise have, knowing that she was a from a family who was already deep within the criminal world — even if she wasn't aware of it.

"Good evening," he said, sneaking up behind her now in the drawing room, where they were assembling before dinner. He was thrilled at the tremor he felt shake her at his voice in her ear, and he couldn't help but allow his mind to take him back to that morning in the cave.

"You look lovely tonight, although not quite as beautiful as in the attire you were wearing this morning," he teased, his voice low enough that no one but she could hear him, although he wouldn't speak of anything that would give them away.

Grace cleared her throat before turning around to look at him.

"I am perfectly fine, yes, thank you," she said louder, a knowing smile of her own on her lips.

By the time they had dressed, the water had begun to recede, and they had slowly made their way out of the cave and back up the cliff. Damien still wasn't entirely pleased with what he had found within the cave, knowing that there was more to be discovered somewhere else, at some other time, but he was replete in the connection between him and Grace and that was what currently mattered most.

Come the time when he had to face Arie, that might change. But for now, it would do.

When they had neared the top, Damien had urged Grace to go ahead in case anyone was observing them, promising that he would watch his timepiece for a good half hour to ensure that no one saw them coming up together, or so soon after one another.

He had been surprised to find that when he entered the

house, not only did his sudden presence not seem to upset anyone, but Grace was calmly sitting at the breakfast table, her hair arranged in the pins the two of them had hastily refastened inside the cave.

Her mother was just coming down the stairs, informing them that they had missed her husband and the rest of the men, who had already left for the warehouse.

"He said something about you joining them tomorrow, Mr. Hondros," she said, waving her hand in the air. "But for today, you really should enjoy Dover. Grace, you must show him around."

And so began another day of exploration. Grace had introduced him to everyone he had already seen as well as those he hadn't met on their previous walk through town. She had taken him to the inn for lunch, they had visited shops that she remembered from previous years and others that were new. They stood back and revelled at Dover Castle high above them, listening to the tools clang away from the fortifications that were currently being added for the potential of an invasion from France — either now or in years to come. It was a chilling thought, but Damien insisted that, from what he knew, it was not likely to happen any time in the near future.

"Besides," he had leaned down and whispered in her ear, nipping at the lobe, "I shall be here to protect you."

"From a cannon?" she had snorted, and he nodded.

"Even from a cannon."

They had also, of course, stolen a good number of kisses anytime they could find a secluded place hidden from view. Damien couldn't remember the last time he had kissed a woman on more than one occasion, let alone snuck off with her to enjoy such time alone.

He had never been quite so happy before.

That her family had even seemed to accept him just made everything better.

"Hondros," her father said now, crossing the room, his face set as he looked at Damien, seemingly oblivious to his daughter's presence.

"Mr. Mulberry," Damien responded with a slight nod of his head. "I do hope you had a productive day."

"My days are always productive," Mulberry responded, not at all modest about his success. Damien had to admit that while Mulberry may not always treat his family — particularly his daughter — in a way Damien respected, the man certainly worked hard and knew how to find success. "One of the reasons I am productive is because I wake early, have my breakfast, and get to work shortly after the sun rises in the summer months. It's something you should learn, Hondros."

"Of course, Mr. Mulberry. I appreciate your advice," Damien murmured, as he attempted to keep his expression even when he saw Grace's face screw up in laughter behind him, for she knew better than anyone that Damien was always awake well before dawn — only this morning, other things had kept him from the breakfast table at such an early hour.

"Well, it's something to work on," Mulberry mused. "My sons and I will speak business with you after dinner, once the ladies retire, all right?"

"That sounds just fine," Damien said, feeling Grace's eyes on him, and when Mulberry walked away, she was staring up at him inquisitively.

"What kind of business does he mean?" she asked, obviously attempting nonchalance, but he could sense the importance behind her question.

"I suppose we shall find out soon," was all he could say, and she looked up at him in astonishment.

"You would actually tell me?" she asked, her eyes wide, and Damien winked at her.

"Have I ever been able to say no to you before?"

Grace's mouth opened and shut, but she said nothing, and Damien grinned at her, pleased that he had managed to find a way to tease her into silence.

Dinner seemed to be typical from the family — the sons and father talking business to one another while Grace's mother spoke to her and Damien, Grace usually nodding and agreeing with her. "It's the best way," Grace had warned Damien before dinner. "Just agree with everything she says and then do what you wish later."

At first, Damien had laughed, until he had realized that Grace could be referring to her mother's desire to see the two of them together. At least after this morning, he had a much better idea of where Grace's intentions lay — hopefully with him.

When Grace and her mother retired, Grace looking back at him with one last quick smile, Damien forced himself to shut off his mind to everything regarding her and focus on business instead.

"Well, now that we have a minute," Mulberry began, "we'd like to ask you a few questions."

"Of course," Damien said, surprised by Mulberry's hard tone. The four men shifted so that they sat across from him, and Damien suddenly felt as though he was in the middle of an inquisition of some sort.

"Tell us more about your brother's interests in working with us," Borden said, obviously feeling himself the next in line to begin discussions, although by Max's hard look, Damien received the impression that the two eldest brothers were in something of an unspoken rivalry as to who was second in their father's empire.

"Well," Damien began slowly, unsure of what exactly they

were looking for. Arie had not exactly been completely forthcoming in his expectations. "Arie has quite a network of connections established throughout London. He is hoping that he can help distribute some of your product after it travels from the docks here in Dover to London."

"Right," Max said, leaning forward, his eyes glinting like steel as he studied Damien. "What if some of that product does not come in on the docks?"

"But through offshore means?" Damien asked, getting to the heart of the matter. He shrugged. "I think due to the nature of our family's other business interests, there wouldn't be any issue in such matters. Our… ethics, as you will, are likely similar."

Max sat back, crossing his arms over his chest. "That is good to know."

"Of course," Damien said with a nod and a small smile, "I would also be interested in learning more about your operations — those that are not in the public eye."

The Mulberrys looked at one another as though trying to silently determine how much they wanted to divulge. Finally Mulberry placed his hands on his rather rotund stomach and regarded Damien.

"We shall take you for a tour tomorrow," he said. "At the moment, most of our ships are at sea and most of the product has already been shipped to London. But we can provide you with a glimpse of what is to come."

"What type of volume do you bring in?" Damien asked, becoming a bit excited himself now at the prospects of their partnership — and Arie's approval that he had brokered such an agreement.

"We already have relationships established to move much of it," Mulberry said, skirting around the question, "but we could use some help with the brandy and cigars."

Damien grinned. "Perfect."

They discussed a few more logistics, with Damien providing as much information as he could regarding what his family may bring to the partnership — storing product and distributing to a network of shops and dealers, in addition to their own purchase of stock. Mulberry seemed pleased with all he said, for when the three bottles of brandy were finished and the night began creeping into the wee hours of the morning, he stood and held out his hand to Damien.

"It's a deal then."

Damien nodded in triumph. It seemed this trip to Dover had been worth more than he ever imagined.

"It's a deal."

CHAPTER 19

Grace thought she had risen early enough the next morning to meet Damien and plan for what was sure to be a day as amazing as the one before it, but she was shocked to find that he was already gone.

"Where is everyone?" she asked her mother when she finally joined her downstairs, her mother having taken breakfast in her room.

"Oh, your father said something about showing Mr. Hondros around the remainder of the operations," her mother said, stretching her arms above her as she yawned. "I'm sure they will be home later this afternoon."

Grace frowned, even though she knew she should be glad that her father at least now approved of Damien. She wondered why he had never mentioned anything to her.

"It must have something to do with the potential partnership his brother had proposed."

"Oh, yes, your father seemed quite smug about it last night," her mother said with a laugh, kicking her feet up on the sofa. "Said something about how it will help further the company's prospects in London, bringing in revenue unlike anything he's ever seen before."

"How much is he talking about?" Grace asked, and her mother smiled like a satisfied cat now.

"Well, he said we could potentially look into moving into a larger townhouse, finally hire more servants," she said. "So possibly much, much more. Show those old rich who have done nothing for their money that their little societies are not quite as exclusive as they might think."

Her mother opened the newspaper in front of her with a flourish and Grace turned away, unwilling to enter into such a conversation. Besides, she was too riddled with questions, most of them surrounding the fact that Damien had not confided in her — but why?

She decided that she could both distract herself and learn more about the company by seeing to the ledgers her father had entrusted her with, and she let herself into the house's small library, where the windows overlooked the sea and she had a small desk where she could work without interruption. She had no trouble with balancing the accounts until she reached the operations that originated here in Dover. She wasn't sure what Max had been doing with his records, but none of it made sense — there were expenses that didn't add up, product that seemed to have been lost somewhere, and extra revenue that had no explanation. She bit her lip as she studied it, realizing that there were only a few ships listed — just as she had noticed at the docks. It was as though a large portion of the operations had been swept away. And yet, her father had talked about nothing lately but additional success.

She sighed, shutting the ledger in front of her. She didn't want to ask her father about the discrepancies, for he would likely only say that she had made a mistake and that it wasn't a job for a woman anyway. Perhaps Max could provide her with some information.

As Damien was gone and the day was bright and sunny, Grace didn't see why a walk wouldn't do her some good. Sure, she could just wait for Max to return home, but what else did she have to do all day? She was too on edge to read, so she decided instead that she would take her ledgers and go down to the company's warehouse.

And if she happened to see Damien along the way? Well, that would just be an added bonus. She told her mother where she was going, pleased that, at the very least, here in Dover she didn't have to take as much care in proper chaperoning — not that she usually did in London. Besides, her mother, as a woman who was raised in London's Covent Garden, did not have any particular rules on propriety as did many of the other women of society. For that, Grace was more than glad that they were *not* part of the elite her mother continued to eschew as much as she wanted to join them.

Which meant that she was rather disappointed when she reached the docks only to find that they were rather deserted. There weren't even any ships in her family's harbour, only a few down the way bobbing in the waves. Grace placed her hands on her hips as she entered the building, not finding Max but only a few workers who didn't seem to be doing much at all.

Her quest fruitless, she was just leaving when she saw the five of them — the five men who now meant the most to her out of any in the world — emerging from down the beach, past the docks. What in the…

She waited, not altogether patiently, until they noticed her. She first saw Damien's smile, followed by Max's frown and her father's disapproval. But why?

"Grace," her father greeted her first. "What are you doing here?"

She bristled at his tone, not appreciating him chastising her in front of Damien and her brothers.

"I actually came with a question for Max," she said, her smile frozen on her face as she lifted the ledger in her hands.

"For me?" Max said, obviously not understanding, and she nodded. "Very well," he said, "come in."

Seeing no other recourse but suddenly feeling very awkward, as though she was somewhere she was not supposed to be, she followed him into his sparsely decorated office before sitting in front of his shiny desk while he looked at her warily.

"What do you need?"

"Splendid to see you too, brother," she said, making her equal annoyance clear, but it didn't seem to matter to Max. Which was typical. Max never seemed to have much care for anything besides business matters. "I am not sure if Father informed you, but he asked me to look after the ledgers."

That got Max's attention. "Did he now?"

"He did," she confirmed. "And this morning I noticed quite a few discrepancies — but only with the Dover docks."

"Are you suggesting that I have not been keeping proper accounts?" he asked frostily, and she shook her head.

"Of course not. I am aware that you are quite proficient at your work here," she said. "However, I thought perhaps you could help explain what is wrong with the books."

She hefted the ledger in front of her on the plain mahogany desk, and Max's eyebrows rose a good inch.

"You carried that all the way here?"

"I did."

"Impressive," he murmured.

"Thank you, but I would rather that we take a look at what's within them."

"Very well," Max said, turning the book around and following her finger and spoken explanation. He finally sat back, rubbing his forehead. "I think you best ask Father about the discrepancies."

"Can you not tell me?" she challenged, hoping to provoke him into making things easier and providing her what she needed to know.

"I cannot," he said, "for this is something only Father should speak to you about. If he wanted you to keep track of the ledgers, then he should properly explain them to you."

"But Max—"

"No protests," he said holding up a hand. "I'm sorry I can't help you."

He stood, a sign that their audience was obviously over. "I'm sorry you came all this way without receiving the answers you wanted, but there's nothing I can do about it."

"There's nothing you *want* to do about it," she said, sensing that he was hiding something — something that he didn't want to tell her, but was leaving for their father to do. Grace was already aware that he never would.

"I'm sorry, Grace," he said, and at least his apology seemed sincere. "I'll see you later. Oh, and Grace?"

"Yes?" she said, hoping he had changed his mind at the last moment.

"Hondros seems to be a good man," he said, nodding, his eyes intent on her. "I'm happy for you."

"Thank you," she said, glad that at least something was finally going right, equally pleased when she found that Damien was waiting for her outside of the building.

"Your father, Borden, and Jeremiah already began their return," he said, "but I told them I would wait for you."

"You didn't have to," she said, secretly thrilled, however, that he had anyway.

"I know," he said with a returning grin.

He walked over to where his borrowed horse was tied to a rail, took the heavy ledger from her hands and placed it in the saddlebag, but then made no effort to mount, instead leading the horse along beside them as they walked back through town.

"Did you get whatever it was you needed?"

"No," she said, hearing the annoyance in her words. "To be honest with you, I feel like my father and brothers are hiding something from me."

"Such as?"

"Something to do with the business," she said with a sigh, before explaining to him the discrepancies in the ledgers. "Max told me that I should ask Father. What type of explanation could there be that he wouldn't want to share with me?"

Damien was silent for a moment, her gaze at their feet, and she turned her head sharply toward him.

"You know."

"I—" he began, but his hesitation and the fact he wouldn't look at her said more than his words could.

"Damien," she cried out. "What is it?"

"Maxwell is right," he finally said. "You should ask your father."

"You cannot be serious," she said, unable to look away from him, his chiseled profile showing his bent nose, his features full of character and saying everything about who he was. "You won't tell me either."

"It's not for me to tell," Damien said, more gently now as he turned to look at her. "It has to do with your family, Grace, and I don't want to get involved in that."

"Yet you don't seem to have any problem in getting involved with them when it comes to your own interests," she said hotly, hearing the accusation in her words but unable to stop them anyway. "What matters more to you — your connection to them or to me?"

"They are one and the same," he said, but then immediately snapped his mouth shut, obviously realizing that he had said the wrong thing.

Grace stopped, and Damien walked a few steps forward before he even noticed.

The realization washed over her like a cold bucket of water, and all of her senses became so focused on what was exactly in front of her that she nearly forgot all else.

"Grace?" Damien said, rushing back, invading her presence one more. "Are you hurt?"

"You— did you get close to me only so that you could become involved with my family's business?" she asked, the words sounding hollow and echoey even in her own ears.

"No!" he said immediately. "Of course not."

"And yet… it all seemed to work out perfectly for you," she said. "Your invitation to Dover, the fact that my father began to trust you after you saved me. None of that would have happened had you and I not come to know one another better."

Another thought occurred to her, one that caused her belly to flip over within her.

"Do you even like going to the bookshop, or was this all part of some elaborate ploy to meet me?"

It all began to make sense. She had always wondered just what he saw in her, why a man like him would want to be with her. He didn't. It was all some ruse, like the other schemes his brother concocted in order to get what he wanted.

"Grace," Damien said, placing a hand on her arm, despite the fact there were now more than a few people watching them. "It's nothing like that," he insisted. "Nothing at all. I *do* enjoy the bookshop. It's the only place where I can find peace. It was fortunate that it brought the two of us together, and not because it meant anything to my family's business interests, but because it brought me to you."

"But—"

He stopped her with his look of desperate hope. "I like

being with you, Grace. I enjoy your wit and conversation, your imagination and your care. How many times do I have to tell you that? I am the one who is lucky to be with you. I am nothing more than a man who speaks with his fists and does the bidding of his brother."

She tilted her head, her mind working as she realized that it might not be he who had manipulated the situation. "It's your brother, isn't it?" she said slowly. "He's the one who wants this connection, who is using what we have to further his own interests."

Damien grunted. "You wouldn't be entirely wrong."

Grace frowned, watching his face for any hint of artifice, but it seemed that she had determined most of the answers she had sought for herself.

"Did he orchestrate this, then, or did you truly meet me by accident?"

"By accident. I swear to you, Grace," he said. "Afterward, Arie saw the opportunity for a partnership between our families. I promised him I would speak to your father about it, but that's it. I don't care if none of that happens, Grace. All that matters is you and me. The rest is just extra."

He seemed so earnest, his face so open and honest, that Grace couldn't help but believe him — even though she knew, deep within, that was exactly what he wanted her to do.

"All right," she said, taking a breath, her lips slightly curling up at the corners. "If you say so."

"I do."

They had just rounded the corner, and before Grace even realized what he was doing, he had swept her into his arms, shielded her away from prying eyes, and showed her exactly what he thought of her.

CHAPTER 20

The week in Dover was everything Damien could have asked for, everything that he had never known he wanted with a woman — or her family. He had only known one family his entire life, and had always felt blessed that Arie had taken him in and provided him with such a home.

None of that had changed — but it was also eye-opening to see the inner workings of a family of another sort.

And then of course there was Grace. She had changed everything.

Damien could hardly believe his luck that he could spend time with a woman like her, let alone consider a future with her. Nearly all her hesitancy had fallen away, although he was aware that it was easier for both of them to forget his past while they were here, in a place where everything was idyllic and he had no work to concern himself with besides that which included her own family.

He was also aware that she had never gleaned any additional information from her father, although she seemed to have accepted Damien's request that he not be the one to tell her and for that, he was grateful of her trust.

But of course, every good thing must come to an end, and now here they were, back in London. When Damien had said goodbye while departing the carriage, her parents had been present and he couldn't exactly say it how he would have liked to, but the small squeeze of her hand and the promise that he would see her soon was hopefully enough to ensure her that none of his intentions had changed.

Of course, Arie had been thrilled with his report and was now clasping his hands together in delight.

"So everything went exactly as planned," he said with a grin.

"Well, I wouldn't say that much of it was planned," Damien argued before taking a breath, hoping Arie would understand. "Grace... Arie, she's everything."

Arie waved a hand in the air, effectively dismissing Damien's intimate confession. "Damien, your women come and go. You know that."

"She's different," Damien said softly, and Diana looked at him with concern, perceptive to the change in his emotion.

"Be that as it may," Arie said, his usual disregard for emotional ties apparent, "you have the trust of her family and that's what matters. Did they agree to meet with me?"

"They did."

"And what did you find out of their operations?"

"In addition to their legitimate business in Dover, they toured me through the caves they utilize beneath the cliffs of their home."

"Which they use for smuggling."

Damien nodded, unable to stop himself from thinking of his first foray into the caves and what it had led to. The second visit was perhaps more informative but far more uneventful.

"It's well situated. The docks are near to the beach where they bring in the small boats. On those boats is the merchandise that they store in the caves. They can access it through a few methods, but the main entrance, the dry entrance, is underneath their own home so there is little chance of others stumbling upon it. The water entrance is well hidden, but leads within to dry ground. The product can only be stored for a short amount of time or it becomes too damp. From there, they remove it through another network of caves until it's above ground, where they transport it on wagons to London."

"How do they ensure they are not caught?"

"They have security, and legitimate product that they use to hide the smuggled goods."

"That's rather ingenious," Arie said, leaning forward, rare respect in his eyes. "And they feel we can provide the connections they need in London to distribute the product?"

"Yes. Mulberry is hoping you can get a better price for him as well."

"We shall see," Arie said, before leaning over and slapping Damien on the back. "You've done well."

Damien nodded, pleased at the praise although tense as a bit of unease coursed through him, as though he had done something wrong, although what, he didn't know. He had been as honest with Grace as he could, and the fact that it had all worked out in both regards was nothing to be concerned about — was it?

"Set up the meeting this week if you can, before Mulberry has other ideas," Arie said, to which Damien nodded, considering that, at least, it might give him another reason to see Grace again. As it was, he was supposed to see her that evening. He had promised her he would meet her in the mews in front of her house. Perhaps all they would do was sit on a bench and talk, but seeing her face would be enough for him.

"Another thing," Arie said, and Damien nodded. "Get dressed. I need you."

"For what?" Damien asked, ready to protest that he already had plans.

"I have a job. A quick job. I'll be in and out. We have to go to Pall Mall, as there is to be an auction tonight for a priceless Greek statue that has come on the market."

Damien's heart fell. When it came to Greek statues — Greek art or artifacts of any kind — Arie was of one mind, and one mind only. It was all to be reclaimed and sold to Greek buyers, who would return it back where it belonged — to their homeland.

Damien, of course, had no argument with that. He only wished it was at a time that wouldn't lead to him breaking his promise to Grace.

"Does it have to be tonight?" he asked, and Arie, who had already risen and was beginning to button his waistcoat, shot him a hard look.

"Of course. The auction is tonight. The statue will be in the building. Before and after that, I have no idea where it might be located. If all goes well, you won't have to do anything. I will pose as a buyer, be in and out in no time at all. You and Diana will be there to look out and ensure nothing goes wrong. If something does, well, that's where you come in."

Damien nodded. It was a familiar plan, and often Arie was right — nothing went wrong and they would be on their way in no time. But one never knew for sure.

"What time do we go?"

"As soon as we can."

"When will we be done?"

Damien jumped when Arie slammed his fist on the table as he turned around to face him.

"What is with all of these infernal questions? We will be done when we are done. You know that nothing else is more important than this, so will you stop the impertinence?"

Damien narrowed his eyes at Arie's outburst, not exactly thrilled with being spoken to like he was a recalcitrant child, but he knew now was not the time to push Arie. It would only make matters worse.

He would try to get a note to Grace. But he had an uneasy feeling that he would have much to make up for.

* * *

GRACE LOOKED in the foyer mirror one last time, ensuring that the curl fell from her forehead just right. She knew she was being ridiculous — Damien had seen her many times before, and it wasn't as though his opinion of her was going to change by how she looked today. She was not typically a woman who tarried over her appearance, but this was the first time she had seen him since Dover. Even though they were the same people they had all been last week, somehow returning home changed their perspective on everything, and she could admit it to herself now — she didn't want to lose him.

She could only hope that his interest would remain.

She still had a niggling doubt that there was something more to his pursuit of her, but she had resolved to be happy with the fact that even if other circumstances and reasons had brought them together, he had sought her because of who she was, and the two of them had found happiness with one another.

She had never thought marriage would be for her but now, having met Damien, her perspective had changed.

Grace fought down the flutter of butterflies in her stomach, taking a breath as she opened the door, disappointed when Damien wasn't waiting for her on the bench in the middle of the square as he had promised.

Well, it didn't matter. If he was a few minutes late, so be it. She could wait.

An hour later, when she was still sitting there with no sign of him, her attitude had changed.

For she had to resign herself to the fact that he simply wasn't coming.

* * *

"Do you know, I don't think you have turned a page in the past ten minutes."

Grace flicked her eyes up to her brother. Jeremiah stood in the doorway, leaning against the frame. Grace bit her lip, knowing that he was right — she had not only completely missed his presence, but she couldn't have told him what the book was about, let alone the words that had just passed in front of her eyes.

"Thinking about him, are you?" Jeremiah asked, walking deeper into the room and taking a seat, looking rather ridiculous in their mother's French bergère pink and white armchair.

"No," Grace said stubbornly, returning her eyes to the words in front of her, but Jeremiah, while not usually particularly motivated by much in life, was relentless when it came to harassing his siblings.

"He's a good chap," Jeremiah said, looping a leg over the arm of the chair, spinning his foot around. "Not what I pictured for you, though."

Grace, already rather irked at Damien for allowing her to sit in the park alone like a fool, waiting for him for over an hour, raised her eyes to Jeremiah, wondering where he was going with this. "What does that mean?"

"I always saw you with the bookish sort. A rather quiet man who would sit with you in front of the fireplace, speaking about literature and all those bluestocking things you like long into the night."

Grace couldn't prevent the picture that formed in her mind of she and Damien doing exactly such things, but she wasn't about to tell Jeremiah that. Somehow she preferred to keep the Damien she knew — the one who enjoyed bookshops and romance novels — as her little secret.

"And you don't see Damien as the sort?" she said instead, to which Jeremiah let out a bark of laughter.

"The fighter? The fists for his family? The man who has spent his life living off the gains of others? Hardly." He stood, making his way to the door, chuckling as he went. "Hondros. Bookish."

Jeremiah hadn't quite made the doorway when the heavy footsteps of their father came thundering down the hall.

"Odd," Grace mused. "Father is never home at this hour."

"Jeremiah!" he bellowed, and Jeremiah jumped before looking around the drawing room as though he could find somewhere to hide. Grace covered her smirk behind her book.

Their father filled the doorway, his eyes glancing at Grace first and then Jeremiah, who had begun to slink backward behind the huge statue that stood next to the fireplace.

"There you are. I've been looking everywhere for you."

"I've been here," Jeremiah said, spreading his hands wide, and despite her annoyance at her brother, Grace didn't give away the fact he had only just walked in.

"We've trouble," her father said. "We need everyone's help."

Jeremiah nodded, grasping the severity of his father's

tone, and Grace immediately sat upright. "What sort of trouble?"

"Nothing for you to worry about," her father said, waving his hand at her, but when he closed the door behind him and a disgruntled Jeremiah, Grace narrowed her eyes. She was not going to be put off like that. She was an intelligent woman who could likely help the situation, if only they would let her. Ready for a distraction, she put her book down and crept to the door, following along the hall to where she could hear her father talking. Eavesdropping on him did not exactly require stealth, for one could hear him bellowing throughout the entire house.

"Someone has learned about our operations and has snitched," he said, his footsteps accenting his words as he must have been pacing. "We have the Crown breathing down our necks. Max is doing everything he can in Dover to make sure there are no signs of any of the secondary business, but we have to be careful that all of our supply here in London is kept secret. We cannot be caught but we can also not afford to lose all of the product."

"Who do you think talked?" Borden was here too. This wasn't a good sign, Grace mused as she wondered what secondary business they might be discussing. "Could it have been Hondros?"

Grace's eyebrows rose at the question in his voice, and despite her current irritation with Damien, she knew he would never betray her or her family like that. She nearly opened the door to the study and told them all exactly that, but she was aware that doing so would not help anything.

"I don't see why he would," her father replied. "He has nothing to gain by turning us in but everything to lose. Our entire deal would be finished, which he obviously so desperately wanted."

Desperately wanted?

"But who else would know?" Borden pushed, and Grace felt a rising panic in her chest at their various opinions over not only their business, but her life.

She walked away from the door, knowing one thing only — she had to talk to Damien. He would have an explanation for everything. Or at least he'd better.

CHAPTER 21

Damien was in a foul mood. The messenger had returned, telling him that he not only didn't make it to Holborn in time, but he had lost the note and had no idea what it said so wouldn't have been able to deliver the message to the lady anyway.

Which meant that Grace had been waiting for him, alone, and now would be irked and likely questioning herself and why he hadn't bothered to show up for her.

Not only that, but he was standing at the back of an auction hall, watching bored people who had nothing else to do with their time but bid on objects that should never be theirs to start with.

"An Egyptian artifact now," Diana murmured as another came across the stage. "Splendid."

"How long did Arie say he'd be?" Damien muttered in her ear, and Diana shrugged.

"You know Arie," she said in a soft tone so that those nearby wouldn't be disturbed or hear their conversation. "He'll tell us what he thinks we need to know when he thinks we need to know it. He didn't give me any additional information."

"Me neither," Damien said, pulling out his pocket watch once more, wondering if he could still get to Grace's and apologize before it was too late in the evening.

"And now, a statue akin to the collection Lord Elgin recently brought to London," the auctioneer began, and Damien stood up straighter, knowing that if there was going to be any trouble, it would begin now.

The auctioneer paused, looking to the side of the room, a frown deepening his cheeks.

"One moment," he said awkwardly, holding up a finger before he disappeared into an adjacent room.

Damien and Diana shared a grin. Arie had done it.

The auctioneer returned to the stand, clearing his throat. "It seems that we shall have to wait on that item, but not to worry, we have many more items of note!"

A murmuring began throughout the room, just as Arie's low voice sounded from behind them.

"Time to go."

Damien and Diana nodded, turning to follow him. He was without the statue, but they knew he would have stashed it away by now. They were nearly at the entrance when it was blocked by a big brute of a man.

"Need to check you," he grunted, and they all looked at one another in some disbelief. Where did he think they would have stashed away a three-foot high statue? Nevertheless, they lifted their arms and turned around, not wanting to make any trouble or bring attention to themselves unless it was absolutely necessary — which, so far, fortunately, it wasn't.

"Fine. Go," he said, nodding toward the door, and when they stepped out into the chill of the night air, Arie clasped his hands behind his back, looking rather pleased with himself. "A fine evening," he said. "A fine evening indeed. Ah, here's the carriage."

They followed him up, nodding approvingly when he opened the hidden hatch in the seat and pulled out the statue, turning it this way and that. "Beautiful, isn't it?"

Damien nodded. He appreciated Arie's sentiments, but had never been quite as passionate about the artwork as Arie. His siblings all had their preferences, but had never been quite the same with his regard for any of it.

They were not far from home and when they pulled up, Damien noted a figure walking up the path toward the door.

"Grace," he breathed, disembarking from the carriage before it had even pulled to a stop.

"Grace!" he called now, and she turned to him, her expression not exactly one that brokered much hope in his chest, but at least she was here. The fact that she had taken the time to find him must mean that she still cared.

"So there was something more important that came up," she said, looking past him at Arie and Diana, who were walking up to the house.

"I'm very sorry, it couldn't be helped," Damien said. "I tried to get a message to you, but apparently it failed. I hated thinking of you sitting, waiting, but Arie—"

"Arie needed you," she said, her voice eerily calm as she nodded. "I understand."

Damien's siblings had joined them now, although neither of them seemed to realize that he would much prefer some time alone with Grace. They were far too inquisitive for their own good.

"I see you were purchasing some art," she said, nodding to the statue, and Arie grinned.

"You could say that," he said, to which Grace's eyes narrowed.

"You stole it, then?"

"We did," Arie returned without any shame. "As a matter of fact, it is rather heavy. If you'll excuse me for a moment."

He placed it within the entrance of the house before waving them in, but Grace shook her head.

"I'm not coming in. I just had to ask you something."

"Of course, anything," Damien said, although he was well aware that Arie and Diana were not far from the door, likely listening to the entire conversation. He gritted his teeth.

"You don't have anything to do with some potential threat to my father's business, do you?" she asked, and Damien lifted his brows in surprise, wondering what had happened and to which part of his business.

"I'm not sure what you're talking about."

"My father and my brothers — they were livid tonight that someone has apparently reported them to the Crown. For what, I have no idea, but Borden suspects that you might have something to do with it."

"Of course not," Damien said earnestly, stepping toward her and taking her hands in his. "I would never do anything to hurt you or your family, Grace. You must know that."

She bit her lip, looking down, and Damien's heart ached at the thought that she might have such distrust in him.

"I know. I was nearly sure of it, but I had to ask. Between that and not seeing you tonight, I was just... I needed some explanation."

"Well, you have it," Damien said, relieved that she seemed to have forgiven him. "I was helping Arie with something that I couldn't leave him to do alone. But I will come see your father tomorrow, to ask what I can do to help. How is that?"

"That would be kind of you," she said, although the worry on her face remained. "Thank you."

"Did you walk here alone?" he asked, looking around, not pleased at the thought, but then was somewhat grateful when she motioned down the street to a carriage and the footman, William, who waved at him.

"I better go before Father returns and requires the carriage," she said, squeezing his hands, looking up at him with a grateful smile that warmed his heart. "Thank you. And I'm sorry."

Damien watched her nearly run down the walk before he turned to the house, colliding with Diana when he did so.

"She's a sensitive one, now, isn't she?" Diana said cryptically, and Damien frowned at her as they continued inside together.

"That's enough."

"She's right, though," Arie said, walking into the room as he counted bank notes in his hand, not looking up at Damien. "It is your fault."

"What is my fault?" Damien demanded, unease shooting through him at Arie's words.

"The fact that her father is facing prison, ruination, or the noose."

Damien could only stare at him in disbelief. "I've done nothing but try to help her family."

"And gain information about them."

"Only for you!" Damien didn't like the look on Arie's face, and he narrowed his eyes at him as he advanced toward him. "Arie, what have you done?"

Arie said nothing as he continued counting, laying the notes on the table as he went.

"Arie!" Damien growled, sweeping the money off the table and onto the floor. "I asked you, what have you done?"

Arie stopped, his hands still held out in front of him. "My, my, but it seems the usual stoic Damien has been riled up."

Damien just waited, not willing to play Arie's games at the moment.

"Fine, fine, very well. Let's just say that our plan has

worked perfectly. At this moment, the authorities are learning about Mulberry's little smuggling operation. They will go in, arrest him, shut down his illegal operation, and leave a hole in demand. That is where we step in and fill it."

Damien could only stare at him in horror. He heard Diana breathe in sharply behind him, and he looked back at her, wondering if she had known, but even she seemed shocked by Arie's scheme.

"*You didn't*," Damien said, his voice just audible enough for his siblings to hear. "Arie, how could you?"

"How could I not?" Arie shrugged. "The man should know better than to allow outsiders into his business. I never have, and therefore have never had such a problem."

"He will be hanged!" Damien exclaimed. "You're going to kill Grace's father."

Arie was still nonplussed, pouring himself a drink as Damien spoke. "Everyone is someone's father or brother or son," he said. "He should have thought of that when he got into this business."

Damien began to pace around the room, swiping a hand across his brow. "She'll never forgive me," he muttered.

Diana added rather unhelpfully, "No, she won't."

"What am I supposed to do?" Damien burst out, flinging his arms wide, but no one seemed to have an answer for him. He turned to Arie. "This is going too far, Arie. You have to stop this. We can make a good business by working *with* Mulberry, not against him. We need to help him get rid of all of the evidence. It's the least we can do."

"I don't think so," Arie said, shaking his head at Damien. "The plan is working out beautifully. Why ruin it now?"

Damien snorted at him in disgust before he was out of the room, already calling for his horse to be mounted. If his brother wouldn't help him, then he had to take it upon himself to save Grace's family.

* * *

By the time Grace arrived home, her father and brothers were gone, her mother in the corner, weeping.

"Mother?" Grace rushed toward her, coming to her knees at her side. "What's wrong? What has happened?"

"Your father is doing all he can to save the business, but Grace, I just don't know… he says that all could be lost."

"I don't understand," Grace said, utterly confused, although she was aware that her mother likely wouldn't be any help. "What could Father have possibly done that would get him into any trouble?"

"He wouldn't tell me," her mother said, tears beginning anew, "but I have never seen him so frightened before."

Suddenly the door flew open and Borden rushed in, kicking off his wet boots.

"Borden, what is happening?" Grace demanded, rising to her feet and walking toward him, but he shook his head slightly as he motioned toward their mother.

"Nothing to worry about, Mother, all is well," he said, before tilting his head in the direction of their father's study. Grace followed him in, already tugging at his sleeve, urging him to tell her more.

"What is going on?" she demanded.

Borden sighed, ignoring her, but Grace knew him and was sure he would come around to sharing *something* with her.

"Where is the ledger book you were working with?"

"In the library," she said, as he left the room without further explanation, Grace dogging his heels.

"What do you need with it?" she asked, perplexed. "As it happens, I never could get it to balance."

"I know," Borden retorted. "And there is no way that you ever could."

"Now see here, I—"

"Not because of you," he said, pushing open the door of the library and walking over to the small desk she worked at. There lay the book, already dusty from the amount of outside air that filtered through the windows into the library all day. "The numbers that Father and Max gave you weren't right."

"But why—"

"The job was to keep you occupied and to give Hondros a reason to remain close to you."

Grace's mouth dropped open.

"What does he have to do with it? And did you not think that perhaps he might actually want to simply be with *me* without further reason?"

"We had to be sure."

And they never could be. Not with her. The truth was written on Borden's face, even if he would never actually say the words aloud.

She stepped in front of him, her hands on her hips, unwilling to let him pass until she learned the truth.

"Tell me what is going on here, Borden."

"I don't have time right now."

"Borden." She set her jaw, looking up at him with enough determination to make him understand that she would not let this go. "Tell me."

He heaved one more sigh, which was enough, for it told her that he had finally realized he was better off telling her what she wished to know, and then she would let it go.

"The reason that the ledger never balanced is because Father didn't give you the information about the part of the business operating out of Dover."

"Which information?"

"Come on, Gracie, you're smarter than that. Smuggling. We smuggle goods on ships that come into a hidden harbor.

Then we use the caves to hide the goods before transporting them to London."

Grace's jaw dropped open as she stared at her brother, who simply stared back at her, resigned and impatient.

"You know now, all right?" he continued. "But I don't have time to worry about your delicate reaction at the moment, because we need to do all we can to hide all of this when they come to investigate us."

"Is there anything for them to find?" Grace asked, finally managing to find her voice, deciding that she would have to suppress all other emotion until a later time, when she would be able to deal with it.

"Fortunately, we had just moved the goods and most of the ships are out at sea. We have to get word to Max in time, but he'll be able to hide the others with the legitimate fleet. Where we are at risk is the amount of goods we have hidden here, waiting for sale."

"Where are they?"

"In — well, *beneath* — one of Father's warehouses, here in London."

"One that can be found?"

Borden grimaced. "If one is a good enough investigator."

"What are we going to do?" she asked, resolved to help now.

"*We* are going to do nothing. You stay here."

"I cannot stay here and do nothing. I—"

Borden continued on as though she hadn't said anything. "Actually, there is something that you need to be careful about."

"Yes?"

"Stay away from Damien Hondros."

Grace's heart skipped a beat. "What does he have to do with anything?"

Borden's face hardened. "No one suspected us of anything

for years. Then we spend a couple of days showing Hondros the business, and suddenly the authorities are on us? That cannot be a coincidence."

Grace went dizzy, her body lightening, and she somehow felt that her consciousness was beginning to float out of it, looking upon everything from above. She took a breath to try to keep herself in the moment.

"D-Damien knew of the smuggling?"

"Of course he did," Borden said, looking at her quizzically. "He was apparently going to broker a deal between us and his brother so that they could distribute for us. But now it seems the truth is emerging — that he wanted us out of the picture completely so that his family could take over."

"No," Grace said, shaking her head, her fingers flying to the ruby necklace she wore around her neck, one that she knew was ridiculous to wear every day, but that made Damien feel close. "That's not possible."

"It's more than possible," Borden persisted mercilessly. "Now, I'm sorry, Grace, but I have to go. Be careful."

There was nothing more to say as she watched him leave.

CHAPTER 22

Damien's first instinct had been to go to the Mulberry townhouse to see what he could do to repair damage there. But as much as he longed to see Grace, to tell her everything from his own perspective before she could hear it from another, he knew that if he wanted to make amends, he best face her father first.

And her father would most decidedly be at his warehouse.

Damien was aware, from the conversations he'd had with Mulberry, that below the legitimate warehouse was another level, one which housed all of the stolen, smuggled goods, before they were distributed to be sold.

What exactly was there, he had no idea, and he tried to recall how much he had told Arie.

Too much.

Damn it, he should have known better. Arie always had another idea at hand, and he never did anything halfway. If he was going to take over an operation, he would do it wholeheartedly. He had never partnered with anyone before. Why would he start now?

And Damien had served everything up to him.

He couldn't imagine what Grace was feeling. Did she know? Did she feel betrayed? He would only know once he talked to her, but that would have to come later.

He dismounted from his horse, leading it up to the warehouse and tying it outside the front door. He knocked carefully, but when no one answered, he let himself in. He found the place seemingly empty, and he began to look around, wondering if he would hear anyone.

It was the brothers' arguing — a familiar sound — that finally tipped him off.

"You are far too slow."

"I'm going as fast as I can."

"We need another pair of hands."

"Well, there aren't any coming."

"I don't know, I—"

By that time, Damien had crossed the warehouse floor to the small hole in the ground, from where the tips of a ladder protruded.

"Can I help?"

All sound and activity from below came to a halt.

Jeremiah's head poked up from below.

"Hondros."

His normally friendly face was guarded, suspicious, and Damien's stomach churned as he realized they were likely already aware of his involvement in this, warranted or not.

"Jeremiah," he greeted him. "I heard there were troubles, and I wanted to see if I could help."

"I think it's best this was left to family," Jeremiah said cautiously, but before Damien could answer, Mulberry himself came storming out of the office area with a slam of the door.

"Hondros! What do you think you are doing here?"

Damien spun around on his heel.

"I'm here to help. I—"

"What? Here to gather more information to pass on? We could have the magistrate here at any moment, and we have little time to get rid of all this product. But I'm sure you already know all of that."

"I only know what Grace—"

"Grace," Mulberry sneered. "Because of her and her infatuation with you, we could lose everything."

"I hardly think you can blame Grace for any of this," Damien said, his ire rising that Mulberry would think to lay it all at his daughter's feet when he was the one who had brought Damien into the family business. "Grace knew nothing about your smuggling operation."

"No, but if hadn't been for her, you would never have come close to us," Mulberry said. "You fooled her before you fooled any of us, and I—"

"What are you doing here?" Grace's voice cut through the rest of theirs, the pain practically dripping off it.

"Grace," Damien said, hearing the anguish within his voice as he turned to her.

"Haven't you done enough?"

"Grace, I told you to stay at home." Borden appeared now, a cart full of goods extended between him and Jeremiah.

"Stay home, and do what? Wait for the ruination of my family?" She turned to Damien, waving a hand toward her father. "And he's right. This *is* all my fault."

"You cannot say that."

"I can and I will," she said hotly, nothing like the unassuming woman he had first met — and he had to admit, he kind of liked her boldness. "If I hadn't let you in, fallen for your games, then none of this would have happened."

"There are no games," Damien said, stepping closer to her,

wishing that they could be alone, but also needing her family to know the truth of what he was saying. "I never meant for any of this to happen, Grace, I swear it." He looked up and met her father's angry gaze. "I do. Truly. This all began because of what I felt for Grace. Then my brother said he wanted to work with you. I didn't see the harm in that — in fact, I thought it might be a good idea for us to help one another. I didn't know that there was any suspicion of your family until you told me, Grace."

She eyed him with some disbelief. "How could you not know? Words are charming and all, Damien, but actions speak much louder."

"I know that, I do," he said earnestly, reaching out to her, but she stepped back away from him, breaking his heart a little more. "That's why I'm here, trying to undo some of the damage that I unintentionally caused."

"It's too late now," Borden said, eyeing Damien with distaste. "You've done enough."

"He's right," Grace said, turning from her brother back to Damien, her eyes filled with tears.

"Can I speak to you alone, for just a moment?" he asked her desperately, hoping she would under his despair.

She hesitated, and even as Borden stepped up, already shaking his head, she held out an arm to stop him.

"One moment. That's all," she said, filling Damien with some hope. If he could only get through to her, make her understand.

He reached out to take her hand, but she kept it tucked within her skirts, and he had to be fine with her following him across the room, stepping behind a tower of boxes, where they were somewhat hidden from view although still within shouting distance. It hurt him to think that she would assume she might need saving from him.

"Well?" she said, crossing her arms over her chest. "What is it you have to say? You can tell me all you want — that you never meant to ruin my family, that you had no idea what your brother was intending, that you… that you actually wanted me for me, but I should have known it was too good to be true. From the start, I questioned what it was you saw in me, what you could have possibly liked in me that everyone else had apparently somehow missed. I am aware that I'm not exactly a woman who attracts all manner of men, and that you would suddenly happen upon me and be utterly charmed was a daydream, something that happens to other women or in the pages of a novel, but never to me. I know you may not have meant to ruin my father's business, but I also am now aware that from the start, you were only using me to get close to my family."

It was Grace who now wore the despair on her face, and Damien ran a hand through his hair, destroyed that she would think so little of herself, that the mountain of belief in who she was that he had seen her slowly building was now crumbling down — and all because of him. How did he make her understand? How did he find his way back, to lift her up again?

"None of that is true," he said fiercely, wrapping his hands around her upper arms, as he had so many times before. "From the start, I wanted *you*, Grace Mulberry. It had nothing to do with your family or your father's business. My brother saw the potential opportunities and acted upon them, and if I am at fault, it is only because I didn't see through him, that I didn't tell him from the start that even if his interests were noble, I would not play into them. The truth is, Grace, I didn't care if I was going to walk away from this with any interest in your father's operations. All I cared was that I had you."

A tear rolled out of her eye, trickling down her cheek

now, and she blinked her long lashes rapidly to try to chase it away.

"Damien, I don't even know if I can trust you anymore — if anything you are saying is true, or if you are only trying to use me again. I should have known from the start — that the man I thought I knew, the man from the library, was not an actual person. That you are who I first imagined you to be. The fighter. The criminal. Your brother's faithful soldier, through and through." She looked away from him, morose. "Please go."

The words were so quiet, he wondered if she truly meant them, or if she wasn't sure herself whether or not she actually wanted him to.

"Can I see you again? Can we try—"

"No."

Her voice was stronger now, her hands in fists at her sides as she looked him square in the eye.

"I don't want to see you again. I don't want to hear your name mentioned in my presence. I don't want anything to do with you. I wish that I had never met you, and that none of this had ever happened."

He opened his mouth to respond but then promptly shut it again. For there was nothing left to say.

"Very well," he said, his voice quiet. "I'll go."

It took everything within him to turn around away from her, but he knew he had no other choice. For if nothing else, he would respect her wishes. He had done enough otherwise.

He told himself not to turn around, not to look at her again, but then found he couldn't help himself. He took one final glance behind him.

"For what it's worth — I never meant for any of this to happen. I'm sorry, Grace. I truly am."

"So am I," she said, before turning her back to him and

walking away, and he heard her mutter to herself as she rejoined her family, "so am I."

* * *

"You sent the bounder packing, then?" her father said as Grace rejoined them, no longer caring if they saw a break in her composure. "Good on you, girl, although none of this would have happened it if wasn't for your little obsession."

Grace lifted her chin and met her father's expression, narrowing her eyes at him.

"First of all, I did nothing but enter into a courtship, a flirtation if you will. *You* were the one who took Damien under your wing, showed him your entire operation, told him things that you didn't even trust your own family with."

Her father's eyes bugged out as his face turned a purplish shade of red.

"Watch what you are saying, Grace Ellen. I—"

"And you know what? You are no better than him yourself."

Even her brothers' mouths opened wide at that declaration, and when the door opened beyond them, Grace couldn't keep herself from twirling around to see if Damien had returned — although what she would do if he had, she had no idea — but it was only some of her father's workers, likely here to help move product. She turned back to her father.

"Smugglers." She said the word with all of the disgust she felt. "All of you. And hiding it from me. Making me think that I was too stupid to balance the ledgers, when really, you had missed providing some key information. Namely, that you had an entire other operation you hadn't seen the need to inform me about."

"You're right on that," her father sputtered. "There was no need for you to know anything about it."

"Well, now I do, and I have to say I'm disappointed in all of you," she said. "I came to help, but you've made this bed yourself, and you will have to take whatever comes of it."

"Are you defending Hondros?"

"Not at all," she said, squaring her shoulders as she turned around to go. "But neither am I defending you."

And on that, she left.

CHAPTER 23

"Pardon me."

Grace waited patiently until the man behind the desk looked up at her. It didn't appear George was in today. She wondered where Mr. Moon was.

"Yes?" he finally said in a bored tone.

"I was wondering, are you hiring here?"

The man looked around behind her, as though wondering if she was speaking for someone else.

"Here? At the bookshop?"

"Yes," Grace said, her heart beating fast, as Lydia stood behind her, the curiosity seeping off her, but she didn't say anything — not yet. Grace was aware that Lydia would have many questions, but for now, she seemed content in waiting for Grace to do "what I have to do" as she had told Lydia that morning.

"Who are you asking for?"

"For me."

Grace was beginning to run out of patience with the man. She was also beginning to despair of ever finding somewhere

— or someone — that would take her seriously. She was well aware that she did not possess a great variety of skills — at least none that would help her in finding a profession.

One thing she did know was the bookshop and the product it held. Whether that could actually lead to anything, she had no idea.

"I see," the man said, although it was clear that he didn't see much at all. "If you leave your information, I will give it to the man in charge."

"Very well," Grace said with a nod, writing down her name and address before she and Lydia moved farther into the reading room to browse the shelves, even though Grace could barely read a sentence at the moment.

Lydia obviously couldn't contain her questions any longer.

"Are you going to tell me what that was all about?"

"I am looking for work."

"Yes, that much is apparent," Lydia said with a sigh of annoyance. "But why?"

"Why? Because I have decided to provide for myself."

"Last I checked, your family was doing remarkably well," Lydia noted with a quirk of her brow.

It was true. Her father and brothers, despite all that was against them, had managed to evade the law — for now. However, from what Grace had overheard, all quite accidentally, there was still an investigation into them. Her father would have to be careful.

"They are," Grace said now to Lydia, "but I do not care to work for them or with them any longer."

"Why not?"

"I just don't."

"Is it because you don't want anything to do with money earned through a smuggling operation?" Lydia said so innocently that Grace dropped the book she was holding.

"What did you say?" she asked when the thud of the heavy tome on the floor brought her back to the moment.

"I said, is it because you don't want anything to do with money earned through a smuggling operation?" Lydia repeated herself, even though they both knew that Grace had actually heard every word.

"I… How did you know about that?" Grace asked, wide-eyed.

Lydia shrugged, but looked down, pretending that she was searching through titles on a lower shelf, but Grace knew better — she just didn't want to meet her eyes.

Suddenly it all made sense to Grace.

"Borden told you."

"Perhaps."

"*When* did Borden tell you?"

"We have been spending more time together."

"And you never told me how significant this was?" Grace exclaimed, obviously too loudly for they received a few irritated stares as well as more than one shushing.

"You were preoccupied," Lydia said in defense of herself.

"Was this before or after we were in Dover?"

"Both," Lydia said.

"I had no idea it was actually a serious thing," Grace said, more to herself than to Lydia. She truly hadn't been paying attention to everything around her, so concerned she had been with Damien. "I'm sorry, Lydia."

"Nothing to be sorry for, not at all," Lydia said, picking up one of Grace's hands. "As long as you are not sore with me for spending time with your brother."

"No, never," Grace said. "I mean, it's somewhat odd, true, and might take some time getting used to, but if you and Borden are sincere about one another, well I cannot think of another woman I would prefer as a sister."

Lydia squeezed her hand as a smile lit her face. "Oh, I'm so glad. I was worried that this would change everything."

"Nothing," Grace said with an answering smile as she shook her head. Her smile faded, however, as she considered how this conversation began. "But Lydia, how do you feel about the fact that he is so involved with smuggling? That he is making his living on stolen money?"

"It's not stolen," Lydia argued. "It is simply not taxed."

"So stolen from the government."

"Then they shouldn't tax so high."

"Perhaps, but—"

"Nothing to argue about," Lydia said, waving away the disagreement. "It is what it is. Now, to get back to this job business. Just what are you going to do and why do you want to do it?"

"I need to support myself," Grace said. "Whatever happens, I never want to be completely dependent on another person — including my father."

"But if the bookshop doesn't take you on, then what are you going to do?"

"That," Grace said with a sigh, "remains to be seen."

* * *

Damien had no idea why he had come here.

It wasn't his night to fight. He had no preparation, hadn't seen the inside of a boxing ring or even trained in at least two weeks.

All he knew was that he had pent-up energy that he had to expend, and there were only two ways he had ever found that worked to be rid of it.

One was women. But he had no taste for that now — for no one, that was, but Grace.

The other was fighting. So here he was.

He had tried the bookshop. But when he had entered yesterday, he had seen Grace standing at the desk and he knew that the one place where he had always found solace was not his place anymore. Not now that she would be working there. When he had overheard her questioning the front desk clerk, he had, at least, ensured that she would get the job she was looking for. Arie knew the man who owned the shop, so it wasn't hard for Damien to put in a good word. It was the least he could do for her after everything else that he had done to her life.

And then he had been restless, prowling the streets. When he had returned home to eat, Diana had looked him over with concern, imploring him to share with her what was wrong, but he had refused. Arie had studied him knowingly, but didn't seem to care that anything was the matter, which only fueled the rage that had been building within Damien. This was all Arie's fault, and yet Damien knew it was futile to say anything to his brother, for he would be met with nothing but silence, stoicism, that I-told-you-so look that Arie always wore whenever his siblings had come to him with their own accusations.

So Damien had stayed away, and now he found himself pacing the outskirts of the boxing ring, watching Joe Conrad take on Clarence Brown, the one man Damien had yet to meet in a match. He knew Arie had been planning on setting something up for them in the future, but Damien didn't want one of Arie's fixed fights. He wanted to find himself a good fight, one in which he could win or lose for himself, without anyone holding back. Brown was a cheap son-of-a-bitch, and would be the perfect opponent for Damien's current mood, as he would feel no guilt at giving him everything he had.

Joe caught his eye and paused for a moment, astonished,

but Damien said nothing. It wasn't Joe he wanted. They had sparred enough, and Damien knew he could beat him.

So as much as he was cheering for his friend, he grinned smugly when Brown won. The man would be high on the win, would be sure that he could defeat anyone that came his way.

Damien left the match with the rest of the crowd, but instead of following them all into one of the many taverns nearby, he waited outside, his shoulders leaning against the rough brick wall behind him. Brown would come out this entrance. Damien was sure of it. Then he would be off to celebrate his victory.

Sure enough, Brown emerged not long afterward, only he wasn't alone — a crowd surrounded him, all of them equally as enthused. Damien didn't care. He would take on Brown alone or with friends. He had enough rage within him to fuel whatever fight came at him.

"That was a good match," Damien said, pushing himself off the wall as Brown's head whipped around, surprised at the voice that came out of the dark, "for a man like you."

"Who is that, hurling insults out of the shadows?" Brown asked, stepping toward Damien even as one of his followers told him just to leave the complainer be. "Too shy to show me your face?"

"Never," Damien said vehemently as he stepped forward into the dim light. "In fact, I had been hoping to meet up with you one of these days."

"Damien Hondros," Brown said, his eyes widening. "You saw my match, then?"

"I did."

"Seems the training you've been doing with Conrad hasn't helped him much," Brown said before grinning, his teeth shining in the dark, which was cut through only by the light that emerged from surrounding businesses, still open.

"Although it makes sense, for he's used to being told which punches to throw, is he not?"

"What's that supposed to mean?" Damien practically growled.

"Only that I know your brother has been fixing matches," Brown said, stepping up toward him, the challenge in his eyes. "But never with me. For I will never allow someone like you to beat me — orchestrated or not."

"Watch your mouth," Damien said, snapping at him, all of the ire that had been pooling deep within his stomach now rising to the surface, threatening to choke him if he didn't let it out.

"Or what?" Brown said, his eyes gleaming.

"Or I will shut it for you," Damien snarled.

"Go ahead. Give it your best shot."

Before Damien could even consider what he was doing, he was throwing a punch toward Brown's nose. If Grace thought him a brute that was good for nothing more than what his fists could do, then so be it. That was who he would be. If he couldn't be the man she hoped him to be, then he would be the one she assumed him to be.

He didn't care. Not anymore.

And when his fist connected with a thud, it satisfied him to his very core.

He was this man. He knew that now.

Damien landed one more blow to Brown's midsection before the man connected back, his fist meeting Damien's temple, sending black dots before his eyes. He stepped back, shaking his head, before meeting him once more, the two of them circling one another in the dark, a true street fight, something that Damien hadn't been involved in for a very long time. Memories of his youth came rushing back, as did a reminder of the life that would have awaited him had Arie not set him on a different course — although would his original course really be so different from what he was currently doing?

Arie. The same man who had betrayed him.

Another of Brown's blows landed as all of the thoughts invaded Damien's mind. Thoughts that had no business being there — not right now, when he should have been focused on the fight in front of him.

A reminder of Grace and the look on her face when she had told him that she believed he had deceived her, that he had ruined everything, filled his mind, and with a bellow he launched himself at Brown, no longer caring about the rules of boxing — for out here, they didn't matter. All of the emotion he had been pushing down for so long erupted, until he found himself on top of Brown, letting him have all of it — or he was, until Brown's followers finally managed to pull Damien off him, although it took about four of them. Damien did all he could to fight them off, but he was finally stilled by one voice that came out of the darkness, one word that stopped him mid-swing.

"Enough."

Arie emerged from the shadows, walking over to stand in front of Damien, who was trying to catch his breath as the sweat and blood mixed together, pouring down from his temples.

"Well, look who it is," Damien said, even he spit out blood from what he was sure an ample cut within his mouth. "Come to rig the finale, Arie?"

"No more," Arie said before turning to the men beside him. "Take Brown inside. Get him cleaned up. You," he pointed to Damien, "are coming home."

Everything within him rose up to argue with Arie, but Damien found that he could barely form any more words. In fact, everything was turning rather hazy in front of him, and he found that, more than anything else, he needed to lie down.

Home not being overly far, Damien hated that he needed to rely on Arie, but as he rested a hand on his shoulder, limping the entire short walk, he vowed to himself that this would be the last time.

Never again would he depend on this man.

CHAPTER 24

"I see someone has decided to rejoin us."

Damien blinked his eyes open as the sitting room came into focus. Arie sat across from him on the chair they all called his "throne," while Diana was kneeling beside where Damien lay on the sofa, dabbing wet linen on what must be fairly significant cuts, for they stung every time she pressed water on them.

"What were you thinking?" Arie had hardly allowed him to open his eyes before he was standing above him, arms crossed over his chest, disdain seeping out of every pore. "That was one of the stupidest things I have ever seen you do. If I didn't know any better, I would say that you *wanted* to take a beating."

"I needed to get some things out," was all Damien said, not wanting to speak anymore of his reasoning to Arie, when Arie was the cause of it all and the one who he truly, deeply wished was on the receiving end of his fists.

"Oh, is that what you call it?" Arie said with a brow lifted. "I have a crazy thought — did you ever think to just tell me what has you so irked?"

"Like you don't already know?" Damien countered, pushing himself up to a sitting position, one hand on his head, cringing as he did so. "You know what you did, Arie. I don't need to put it into words."

Arie shrugged as he retook his seat. "What's done is done."

"No, it's not," Damien retorted. "We can make this right. We have to."

"And just how do you suppose we do that — if we even wanted to? Which I don't."

"You undo whatever you did. Go to whomever you gave information to. Tell them it was false. That you were under an impression when really it was regarding something else entirely. That there was miscommunication. I don't care what you do, but *undo* it."

"And then what? You'll go running back to your woman and tell her all is good now and that she should take you back into her life? Are you such a fool that you think it might be so simple?"

"Not at all," Damien said, even as grief at the loss of Grace in his life nearly overwhelmed him. "But at least I will know that we have done all we can to reverse the pain that we have caused."

"That's all well and good for you," Arie said, lifting up the newspaper in front of his face. "But it won't be happening."

With a growl and a squeak from Diana as she was set back on her bottom from surprise, Damien was off the sofa, ripping the paper out of Arie's hands. His astonished brother looked up at him, hands remaining in the air as though the paper was still there.

"You better have a good reason for doing that."

"You will do this, Arie," Damien seethed, "or you will join Mulberry under investigation."

"Pardon me?" Arie responded, standing up and looking

Damien square in the face. Damien was taller and broader than he, but Arie had an imposing air that was hard for anyone to deny.

"If you do not ensure that Grace's father goes free on this, then I will take everything I know about you to the magistrate. Everything. The plots, the thefts, the fight-rigging — everything. Including…" Damien smiled wickedly as he said it, knowing that it was Arie's greatest wish. "…your scheme to steal the Greek statues back from the British Museum."

Arie's eyes narrowed so tightly they were nearly shut.

"You wouldn't."

"Watch me."

Damien turned and began to stride toward the door. He didn't know exactly what he would bring as proof, but his word alone, as Arie's brother, could be a start.

He would do it, too. Arie might have done much for him, but he had gone too far this time. He had tried to destroy the family of the woman Damien loved.

For yes, he loved her. And he refused to see such hurt continue for her. He may not be able to win her back, but he would do anything to fix the mess he had created.

"Do you have no shame?" Arie said, his voice eerily calm.

"Not anymore," Damien said, standing his ground. "But that's a question best asked of yourself."

"Get out of my house," Arie said, his expression void of any emotion, but the shaking of the words making apparent the anger he was just holding under control. "And never come back."

* * *

DAMIEN DIDN'T GO to the magistrate.

At least, not right away.

Instead, he began to compile all of the information he had

on Arie, everything that could send him away for years — although it would most likely have him hanged.

Damien was angry, but he would never go that far. He was aware of that, as was Arie.

But perhaps he could convince Arie that he was not backing down. Arie had pushed him this far, had he not?

Of course, he couldn't put it all together as quickly as he would have liked. There was the business of finding himself a room to rent. Of collecting his few meagre belongings when Arie was not at home. Diana had been waiting at the door. She was visibly upset, which was a rarefied occurrence, but there was nothing Damien could do. Not unless Arie agreed to reverse all he had done.

But Arie was too stubborn.

"I know he didn't mean it," Diana had pleaded, even as she brought him a sandwich, telling him that he was going to waste away, which would have been comical in another circumstance, for Damien was about as far from wasting away from any person he knew.

But now wasn't the time for jesting.

Then of course, there was the time spent watching after Grace. He was aware now that she spent far more time than he would have liked walking the streets by herself, and while she might have enjoyed that freedom, it caused him a great deal of consternation. He couldn't forget about the last time he had come upon her walking alone and the danger she had been in.

Unbeknownst to her, he had taken it upon himself to become her personal protector, to follow her and ensure she came to no harm — especially in the evening hours. She usually didn't go far, perhaps to a lecture or to help her father at his building, but Damien didn't think he would ever forgive any of the Mulberry men for allowing her to venture out alone.

So far, she hadn't caught sight of him, which was a good thing, for he knew she wouldn't exactly be pleased to find that she had a shadow — especially a shadow she had banished.

However, he might not be able to be with her the way he wanted to, but the least he could do was ensure that she remained safe, although it would not be for himself, but for the fortunate man who was to come her way in the future.

He couldn't put her out of his mind, not even as he bundled the last piece of information about Arie with the other papers, sliding it all together before adding a note with an address on top. In fact, he had created two copies of the information he had compiled — one to go to Arie himself, and one to be sent to the Mulberrys two days after Arie received his. If Arie didn't follow through and fix this, then the Mulberrys would receive everything they needed to do to Arie what he had done to them.

Damien left the second pile on the table in his room. He looked around at the bare walls, the clean floor, and his few belongings, most stacked tidily across the room. It wasn't much, but it would have to do. The rent was reasonable, the housekeeper kept things clean, and it was close enough to the Mulberry house that he could watch over Grace.

It wasn't home, but he had no other choice now.

Damien's heart was heavy as he approached the townhouse that *had* been his home for so many years now. He knocked on the door, something, he realized, he had never done before. It swung open to reveal Diana, who looked at him wide-eyed.

"Did you forget something?" she asked, her voice somewhat hushed. "Arie is home, but he is leaving."

"No, I forgot nothing," he said. "I actually have a package for him."

Diana looked at him warily. "Is this something he is going to welcome?"

"No."

She held out her hand. "Perhaps it's best I give it to him."

"I'd prefer to give it to him myself — along with a message."

"You don't trust me, then?" Diana crossed her arms over her chest, her expression defiant, but Damien knew better — Diana was hurt and likely more torn apart than anyone by the rift between him and Arie. But he had to put this into Arie's hands. He had to let him know that he was serious, that this meant more to him than anything else.

"Who are you hiding out there?"

Damien and Diana looked at one another with consternation as Arie's voice thundered down the hall, and Diana reluctantly pulled back the door to reveal Damien standing on the step. Arie's gaze instantly hardened.

"I told you not to come back."

"I'm not here to stay," Damien replied in a tone as icy as Arie's. "I came to deliver something to you."

"A gift — for me?" Arie returned sarcastically.

"You could say that," Damien said, even as Diana stepped between them once more.

"Arie, perhaps we should invite Damien in. I'm not sure we should do all of this when anyone could be watching, do you?"

"I don't particularly care," Arie said, his jaw set tightly, his teeth clenched. "He is not coming into my house."

Damien snorted. "A house that is mine as much as yours."

"Watch what you say."

"Fine. Keep your house and your pride. But take a read through this as you do so."

Arie looked down at the papers in Damien's hand but

didn't make any motion to reach out and take them from him.

"Which is?"

"Everything that I will send to the Mulberrys if you don't make things right."

"I told you that's not going to happen."

"Then consider all of this to be public knowledge. At least, if that's what the Mulberrys decide to do with it. Or perhaps they will prefer to take you down with it in other ways. I'm not entirely sure. It will be up to them."

"You wouldn't." Arie's face, normally so stoic, was beginning to turn an odd shade of purple.

"I would," Damien said calmly. "You have two days to decide. If I don't hear from you, I will turn it all over. And not to worry — I have another copy."

He smiled smugly, even though his gut was wrenching, and then turned and walked down the stairs, refusing to look back.

CHAPTER 25

While everything else in her life seemed to be going in the wrong direction, Grace had been shocked — *shocked* — when she had received a letter to meet with a Mr. Edmundson at the bookshop.

She had been even more surprised when he had greeted her with enthusiasm and proceeded to offer her a position.

"Truly?" she had asked, wide-eyed. The truth was, when she had provided them her information, she had never thought she had a chance of receiving any contact from them — especially after her conversation with the clerk. The clerk who had been sitting at the desk when she arrived, who had looked at her warily, as though to tell her that this was not his idea and he certainly didn't approve.

While he would likely be anything but a joy to work with, Grace didn't care. She had work. She could support herself. And, eventually, she might be able to find a place of her own.

"Do you need to see my qualifications?" she had asked him, but he had waved her away.

"You have references enough," he had said, and Grace had stared at him, puzzled.

"I never gave you any references."

"Well, you have them anyway," the man had said, and Grace could tell that he wasn't entirely pleased by whatever mysterious references had been provided. "You can start Monday."

So here she was, sitting rather tentatively behind the circulation desk. She received more than her share of strange looks, and some visitors ignored her altogether, but Grace didn't entirely care. She had work, she had the chance to earn a living, and she was in a place she enjoyed.

She just wondered who had provided her such a reference that would practically give her the job. Her father had obviously had nothing to do with it, for if he had any inkling that she was working, she knew he would likely forbid it.

So she had to make sure he didn't find out — which meant a great deal of excuses and sneaking out. She felt guilty, but she saw no other way. Not right now. It was not as though anyone in her family was particularly attentive to her actions. Her mother should have been, but she had been so distraught upon finding out that her father's business was not exactly as legitimate as it should have been that she had been beside herself in her bedroom all week, certain that she was going to soon have to watch her husband sent to the gallows and then hanged in Tyburn Square.

Grace had tried to explain that no one was hanged at Tyburn any longer, but rather at Newgate — information which hadn't exactly helped matters.

The day went by much more quickly than Grace had thought it would, although once she began it came easier. Her job was mostly focused on the circulation library and the reading room, which she knew as well as her own household. As she already understood the library's systems, it was simply a matter or summoning up the will to speak with most of the people who required her services.

Grace had been surprised when she looked up from her work, long after the bookshop had closed, to find that the sun had already begun to set and night had crept in. She hurriedly packed up her few belongings, aware that it was now likely too late to walk. She probably would have, had it been a few months ago, but she couldn't forget the moment when Damien had saved her, and what could have happened had he not arrived when he did. At the reminder, she realized that today had been the first time, in a very long time, that she hadn't ruminated on Damien and the loss of him in her life every single minute of her day.

She bid goodnight to Mr. Moon, who was closing up with her, and, bag under her arm, stepped out into the early evening, feeling the chill that was just beginning to set in.

Grace shivered as she looked around, convinced that she was being watched. Which was ridiculous. She was just overthinking things.

With no hack visible on the street, she decided she would do best to keep to the busiest of roads possible to reach Leicester Square. She couldn't shake the feeling of eyes on her back, however, which was why she was looking backward when she rounded the corner — and ran right into a figure coming the other way.

"Pardon me," Grace murmured, ducking around the man to go by, when an arm shot out and caught her.

"It's you."

"Me?" Grace exclaimed, surprised. There was nothing particularly interesting about her, and she couldn't think of any reason why anyone might recognize her, unless perhaps they knew her father — but even then, she had remained separated from the business for so long the possibility was next to nothing.

"You." He looked around her, and seeing that she was alone, his lips began to spread in a thin line, and the chill that had been threatening began to creep up Grace's back anew. She took a step back, realizing that she recognized this man — she was just unsure from where that would be.

Until he brandished the knife and she saw the cuts around his nose, and her breath caught. He was the man from the attack. One of the ones who had threatened her when Damien had come along. Grace turned, the only recourse she could see was to run. She wasn't fast but maybe—

When she turned, however, the panic doubled, as her way was blocked by a second man. They must work in pairs, she realized, her heart beating fast, and she began to breathe quickly, her head turning from one side to the other.

"Please let me go," she pleaded, looking at the man. "I am sorry for what happened to you, but I have no control over my... friend."

"He beat us bloody," the other man growled, and hope sprung in Grace's breast as she remembered Damien's threat. It seemed wrong, somehow, to use him to help her in such a situation when she had told him she didn't want to see him again, but at the moment she would do anything to save herself.

"If you let me go," she said slowly, "I promise not to tell him that I saw you again. Or that you threatened me or even said a thing to me."

"How would he ever find us?" asked the first man.

"He can find anyone," she said, forcing strength into her voice. "He's part of the Hondros family."

At the swift intake of breath behind her, Grace knew that the name had caused fear to spring up in the man's breast, and she allowed herself a small sense of triumph.

"I dunno, Jack," the first man said. "Maybe she's right."

"Don't use my name, y'idiot!" The second man said with exasperation. "What does that say about us if we let her go?"

"Tell ya what," the first man said to her. "Give us all you have and you can go."

"I have nothing but a few books," she said, thinking about the ruby necklace she still wore around her neck. "That's all."

The second man — Jack — grabbed her bag and rummaged through it before returning it to her with a snort. "She's right."

"Jewels?" the first man said, and she shook her head, showing her ears and her wrists and fingers.

"Check her neck," Jack said, and the first man roughly shoved her cloak aside, grinning when he found the ruby. Grace swallowed hard to hold back the whimper that threatened when he found her prized possession. He gave the necklace a tug, the chain breaking although not before it bit into her neck for a moment.

"I see ye've been holding out on us," he said, his eyes glinting. "If you were anyone else, you would pay for that. But go on. Get out of here."

Grace placed her fingers against her chest, already missing her last reminder of Damien. But she was no fool — she would not risk her life for a necklace. Before they changed their minds, she picked up her bag and ran.

* * *

STANDING behind the corner and watching the man touch Grace had been the hardest thing Damien had ever done.

But he couldn't take action. Not yet. Because the lesson he was going to teach these men for even speaking to her was something he didn't want Grace to see. He didn't want her to think any less of him than she already did — if that was even possible.

She never would have even seen the men if he had been on time. But the meeting with Arie had held him up and he had been late for the time she was to depart the library, leaving her alone. Damien had been about to step in and intervene, but when he saw Grace bravely set her shoulders and invoke his name, he had waited to see how the rest of the situation would play out.

He had been so proud of her, as she had been so brave, although he hoped that she understood she would not be able to talk her way out of every situation and that perhaps, in the future, she might think twice before walking home alone.

But no matter. It was done now, and he had to make these men understand that when he had told them not to bother her ever again, he had meant every word of it.

He stepped out from the shadows, blocking their path. The men looked up with a start, and Damien smiled in triumph at the fear that crossed their faces.

"Hello, *gentlemen*," he intoned. "Lovely evening for a walk, is it not?"

"We didn't do nothing!" the first man said hurriedly, pointing back at Grace, who was now approaching the square and out of hearing range. "We let her go, just like we said we would. Never touched her."

"No?" Damien said, leaning over him. "I suggest you try not to lie. For I saw the entire exchange and I have to say I disagree with you."

"Just give him the necklace, Jim, and be done with it," the second man said, obviously the smarter of the two in wanting to be as far from Damien as possible before he might begin on the two of them again. "Hurry, now."

"As a matter of fact, I have a connection to that necklace," Damien said, holding his hand out, "as I'm the one who gave it to her."

Even with the men before him and all that Grace had just faced, Damien couldn't help the bit of victory that had raced through him when he had seen the ruby was still around her neck. As Grace was not exactly the type to hold onto jewels for the fact they held great value, he hoped that somewhere, deep within her, part of her still felt something for him — something besides hatred.

But if she couldn't want him — love him — for who he was, then all they had was a memory, and that would have to do for now.

"Jim."

"Fine," the first men said in disgust, before reaching into a pocket and pulling out the necklace, practically throwing it into Damien's hand. "Here you go."

"Come along, Jim," the second man said, but Damien placed his hand on the man's shoulder with a thump.

"Just wait a minute," he said. "Where do you think you are going?"

"We gave you back the necklace," the man said, his eyes widening in fear.

"Yes, but I told you never to touch her, never to speak to her again," he said, all of the anger that had been raging within him — at Arie, at Mulberry, at the fact that he could never be with Grace again — beginning to surface, directed at these two men in front of him who had dared to accost the woman he loved. "You went against that order."

Just as he was deciding what exactly he was going to do to the two of them, he noticed relief enter the man's eyes, and Damien scrutinised him, trying to determine just what might cause him to lose his fear. Then the hairs on the back of his neck began to stand up, and he turned around slowly after he sensed a presence around him.

Only to find five other men, one of them holding a bat, had formed a semi-circle behind him.

Damien swallowed hard. There was no question about it — this wasn't going to end well.

CHAPTER 26

On the two days a week that she worked, Grace had been trying to take breakfast after her father had left for the day, but with enough time that she could still arrive at the bookshop before her shift began.

Today, she was not so lucky. It seemed her father was leaving later than usual, and he and Jeremiah were still at the table when she arrived.

"Good morning," her father said, in a much cheerier mood than he had been of late. Grace knew better than to remark upon it, although it was rather curious.

She was hoping for additional hours at the bookshop, but at this point, she would take what she could get. Besides, her family might not notice her absence for a couple of days of the week — she could always say she was with Lydia — but if she disappeared daily, they would begin to take note.

At least, she hoped they would.

She frowned at the thought, even as she began to add up how many days she would need to work in order to afford her own place to live. She had always been hopeful that one day, she and Lydia might be able to live together, working and growing old together as neither of them had been hopeful in finding husbands for themselves.

But now with Lydia's involvement with Borden, that all had changed. Grace was to meet Lydia later that morning, so she was looking forward to hearing just how everything between them had progressed — and just how serious Lydia believed their attachment to be.

"Is something the matter?" Jeremiah asked as he reached over her for the sugar, and Grace swatted his hand away before passing it to him instead, causing him to grin ruefully at her. Jeremiah had never had the best of manners.

"Nothing at all," Grace said as Borden walked through the door, greeting them before taking his place at the table.

"Borden," she said with some surprise, "what are you doing here this morning?"

"Lovely to see you too, sister," he said with a laugh, just as her father placed his fists on the table, causing Grace to jump as he captured their attention.

"Good, Borden is here now, so we can begin."

"Begin what?" Grace asked, perplexed.

"The most wondrous thing happened," he said, his eyes flashing. "We are going to have our vengeance."

"Our vengeance?" she repeated, knowing that he likely wasn't pleased with her interruptions, but she couldn't help herself. She was too suspicious now, after everything that had been kept from her by all of the men in her life. "On whom?"

"On Hondros, that's who," he said, his eyes darkening as his lips spread into a thin line in his ire.

"Damien?" she said, trying to cover the catch in her voice.

"No, actually. Damien has been *most* helpful. It's because of him we will have our revenge — over his brother."

"I'm not sure what you mean," Grace said, looking around

the table, finding that her brothers seemed similarly perplexed.

"I received a package this morning. It must have come late afternoon yesterday, but to the house rather than the business, so I didn't see it until I rose. It has everything we need in it. Everything Hondros has ever done. Every scheme, ever law broken, every upcoming plan, proof of it all." His eyes flashed. "Now we just have to decide what to do with it."

"But what does this have to do with Damien?" Grace persisted.

"Why, he was the one who sent it," her father said, a statement to which Grace had no retort.

"He did?" Borden finally chimed in. "For whatever reason would he possibly have to betray his own brother like that?"

Jeremiah, never usually one to join such conversations, sat back from the table, folding his arms over his chest.

"There is one reason."

"Which is?" their father asked gruffly.

"He was telling the truth," Jeremiah said. He had always been the one to see the best in people, to give them the benefit of the doubt when everyone else would go against them. "Maybe he did just want Grace. Maybe he did just want to work with us. And then his brother was the one that turned against us — and him."

They were all silent for a moment, contemplating the levity of Jeremiah's words — and the likely truth to them. For there could be no other reason for Damien to send such a package. And Grace had turned him away, had told him that she never wanted to see him again — when he had done nothing but trusted in his own brother, as she would have herself.

She dropped her head in her hands as her stomach turned, and she wondered whether he would ever forgive her. For she had been agony without him. She missed him as she would if a piece of herself had gone missing, and even if this revelation had not come to light, she had begun to wonder if she would be strong enough to never return to him.

Her stomach began to ache as she realized what her own betrayal must have felt like to him, how hard it would have been for him to let her go when he knew that he had done nothing wrong but want her.

Oh, she had been a fool.

Could he ever forgive her?

She had to try. Even if it meant putting herself prostrate before him and begging for his forgiveness.

"I have to go," she said, standing abruptly, putting a halt to the conversation around the table, conversation that she had been completely oblivious to as she had been so distraught over her discovery.

"Where are you going?" her father asked.

"Isn't it obvious?" Jeremiah said with a grin. "She's going to see Hondros."

"Hondros?" he bellowed.

"Damien, Father," Jeremiah said with a sigh.

"Oh," he said more calmly, obviously somewhat mollified. "I suppose that is fine."

Grace didn't care what he thought anymore — about Damien or about whatever she decided to do with her own life.

"I'll be back," she said, pushing her chair in as she began to dart from the room, but then stopped, thinking of something. "Oh, and Father?"

"Yes?"

"Will you make me one promise — please?"

He seemed about to say no, but then finally stopped and considered her — actually looked at her, in a way she couldn't remember him doing in some time.

"What is it?" he asked warily.

"Don't do anything with this information — at least until I return from talking with Damien. Please? Just for this morning?"

Her father rubbed a hand against his chin as he stared at her, until finally, he slowly nodded.

"Very well. Until this afternoon. I need time to think on it, anyway."

"Thank you, Father," she said, and then rushed out the door, nearly colliding with Lydia on her way down the stairs.

"Grace!" Lydia exclaimed. "Where are you off to in such a hurry? I thought we had a day planned."

"We do. We did," Grace said, nearly desperate to continue on her way but knowing that she owed Lydia an explanation. She told her everything that had occurred that morning, as briefly as she could.

Lydia's eyes widened as she spoke, until finally, she was practically pushing Grace down the street. "What are you waiting for, then? Go!"

Grace nodded, nearly running down the street to hail a hack before someone remembered that she should likely be properly chaperoned. But she had no time for that now. She couldn't say what it was that was driving her — love? Guilt? All she knew was that she had to get to Damien. And she had to get to him now.

* * *

Grace was ready for the look of surprise on the face of Damien's sister when she swung open the door to greet her. What she wasn't prepared for was how haggard and tired Diana looked.

"Grace," Diana said wearily. "You must have heard."

"Heard? Heard what?" Grace frowned, wondering if there

had been some falling out within the family now that Damien had released such information. She couldn't imagine Damien's brother allowing him to stay and live with him knowing what he had done, but perhaps Damien hadn't told him yet. He had, after all, kept other secrets in the past.

"Oh, you don't know," Diana murmured, her blue eyes fading into a look of pity that the downturned corners of her mouth matched. "You best come in."

"What's wrong?" Grace asked, immediately on edge, especially when Diana sat her down in the sitting room. The house, which on Grace's one other visit had been fairly pristine, looked as though it had been through a battle itself.

"Diana—" Grace began again, but Diana held up a hand.

"There's been an… accident."

"An accident? Is Damien all right?" Grace asked, her heart beginning to pound.

"He should be," Diana said, biting her lip. "But he's fairly badly injured right now, and—"

"What happened? Where is he?" Grace asked, standing now, her hands in fists at her side as she demanded answers from Diana, no longer caring about manners or Diana's own potential unease.

"He was attacked," Diana said simply, obviously understanding Grace's immediate need for answers. "And he's upstairs in his bedroom."

Grace nodded her thanks, but just as she reached the bottom step, Diana called out, stopping her.

"One more thing."

"Yes?" Grace asked impatiently.

"When you see him… best be prepared to hide what you are truly thinking. From what I can tell, it's worse than it looks, but between the bruises and the swelling…"

Diana didn't need to say any more. Grace was already hurrying up the stairs as fast as she could go, nearly tripping on her skirts in her haste. She couldn't entirely remember which room was Damien's, but Diana must have predicted that, for she called up, "Second door on your right!" just as Grace reached the top.

She threw open the door without knocking, her panic and need to get to Damien overcoming all else.

Then she just stood there, staring.

Damien was on his side, curled around his midsection as though he was protecting injuries. Diana had been right. His face was bruised, while there were lacerations underneath his eyes. His nose was so swollen Grace had to wonder how he could possibly breathe, and there was a piece of linen wrapped around his head.

She swallowed her panic down, trying to keep it within as she slowly inched over to the bed, kneeling on the floor beside where Damien nearly hung over the side.

"Damien?" she said cautiously, and when he didn't respond, she wondered if he was sleeping. A thought overcame her, one she didn't want to entertain but couldn't help herself, and she reached up to check if he was still breathing.

At the moment before her hand touched his cheek, he reached up and grabbed it, his large fingers nearly enveloping her hand, which she didn't think was that small or petite, but in his grasp it seemed to be.

"Grace."

His voice was low, guttural, gravelly, and her heart broke at how much pain he must be in.

"Damien, wh-what happened?"

"Had a little beating," he said, his lip quirking just enough that she could tell he was attempting to smile. "Nothing to worry about."

"Nothing to worry about?" she exclaimed. "Damien, look at you!"

"Haven't had the chance yet," he said. "Thought I would wait 'til I was a bit prettier."

"How many of them were there?" she asked, knowing that it likely didn't matter, but in order to overcome Damien, there would have to be quite a few.

"Seven. And a bat."

"Oh—"

"Most of the injury is to my ribs," he said. "Lucky a runner came along and scared them off. 'Cept now I'm back in Arie's home and he's likely none too pleased. Nice of you to visit."

"That's actually why I'm here," she said, kneeling on both legs before him, so that their faces were even. "My father received your package."

"My what?"

"The package — the one you sent about your brother."

Damien's eyes shot open wider than she had seen them since she had arrived, before he squeezed them tightly shut in apparent pain. "Oh, shit."

"You... you didn't mean to send it?"

"I did — but not until later in the week, if Arie hadn't done as he promised."

"Which was?"

"Make sure the investigation disappeared. Damn housekeeper. Far too efficient."

"My father agreed not to do anything to anyone until I returned from seeing you," she said. "Hopefully, I can get him to give you more time."

Damien sighed. "I've made a mess of things," he mumbled.

"*You* have? Oh no, not at all!" she exclaimed. "It was me. I didn't trust you. I didn't believe in you, when I should have known better. I'm so sorry, Damien. I—I've been terrible to you."

"S'all right."

"It is *not* all right! I know now that you never lied to me, that you were telling me the truth, and I didn't believe you. I *should* have believed you, Damien, should have known that you would never hurt me like that."

He reached out a rough hand and cupped her cheek, stroking his thumb over her skin, and Grace couldn't help but lean into it.

"You just feel sorry for me. But I've gotten what I deserve now."

"Not at all!" she cried, leaning forward until their noses were almost touching, and the tears that Grace had been fighting since she had walked into the room began to roll out of her eyes. "I don't feel sorry for you. Not at bit. For I know that however this happened, you were likely only protecting someone you cared for. That's what you do, Damien, you watch out for those you love. You protect them. No matter the cost — even if it is of yourself. I thought I could live without you, that I was better off on my own, but if I have realized one thing over the past couple of weeks it is that I miss you with an earnestness I cannot even put into words. You are everything I didn't even know I wanted, and not having you near me is like missing a piece of myself. I cannot properly explain it, but I just need you to know that I love you, Damien Hondros. And even if there will never be room for me in your life again, I had to tell you. You are a good man, and I love all of you — every part of you."

Grace was trembling now, and as much as she wanted to reach out and wrap her arms around him, so much was holding her back — his physical injuries, yes, but even the thought of whether or not he would want her to, or if he would only push her away. She had, after all, done the same to him not long ago.

He rose from the bed on one elbow, the strength it took him to do so obvious, but he showed no signs of complaint.

"Truly?"

"Truly."

"Grace." The way he said her name was a caress in itself. "I love you too. More than I can put into words. And I don't exactly have a way with words to begin with."

Grace almost couldn't speak, as her voice caught in her throat, the angst she hadn't realized she was holding onto so tightly rolling off her shoulders.

"It doesn't matter," she finally managed, even though the words he did say mattered more than anything she had ever heard before.

"I'm a man of action. But I don't seem to have the ability to take the action I'd like right now."

"There will be time enough for that later," she said, as they were both trying to find a way to properly embrace, but every time she even lightly touched him, he winced.

"I wish I could find those men and beat them for you," she said fiercely, and he chuckled until that caused him to suck in a breath as well.

"Don't worry about that," he said. "Arie's already on the lookout for them — as is the runner who found me. I'm not sure who I'm rooting for to find them first."

Grace bit her lip, not wanting to think about what Arie would do to them, although she couldn't help the thought that they had what was coming to them for doing this to Damien.

The sun inched down lower through the window, and as it did, it gleamed off something red shining on Damien's bedside table.

"What's that?" she asked, unable to help herself from standing and walking over to it, but when she realized what was sitting there, she couldn't stifle her gasp.

"Damien… this is my necklace."

"It is."

"Where did you get it?" she asked, whirling around, her

heart beating fast. "This was stolen from me just two days ago. How did you—? Oh!" The realization hit her and she could only gape at him. "The men that beat you," she said, her voice just above a whisper, "they were the men who came after me. But how—"

"I'm sorry," Damien said, shocking her by seeming actually ashamed of himself. "I didn't want you to know as I didn't think you would be pleased but I— I followed you."

"From the bookshop?"

"Everywhere," he said. "I was worried about you. I didn't want you to get hurt again, and so I decided that even if I couldn't be with you, I would look out for you."

Grace considered what he was saying — from both his point of view as well as her own. She didn't like the idea of lacking independence, but she supposed she could see where Damien was coming from.

A thought struck her.

"But those two men — you took them on before, with ease."

"I did," Damien said. "But there were more that joined them. Many more. They must have been part of some organized group. I didn't stand a chance."

"Oh, Damien," she said, aching for him and the agony he must have suffered. "I wish you hadn't."

"I'm glad I did," he said, fierceness in his voice that she wasn't expecting. "I would do anything for you. I need you to know that."

"I do," she said, kneeling beside him again, the necklace clasped in her hand. "Perhaps we could come to an agreement. Not quite as much… protection for me, but we will ensure that I am careful. That I am not walking the streets alone. Is that fair?"

"I can agree with that."

"Good," she said, leaning in and landing the softest of

kisses on his lips, one that he likely barely felt but wouldn't hurt the lacerations.

"Grace," Damien said in a low voice. "When I can actually stand, I will do this properly, but I need to know... would you make a life with a man like me? We'd have to find our own way, as it seems we'll likely be on the outs with both of our families, but I offer you all of me, and I promise you, I will find a way to make a life for us."

"Yes," Grace said, placing another kiss, slightly firmer this time, on the one part of his face that was without cut or bruise. "A thousand times yes."

"Except it won't be necessary to find your way alone."

They both looked up with a gasp at the unexpected interruption — and found Arie standing in the doorway.

CHAPTER 27

"Nice of you to finally come visit, Miss Mulberry, considering this was all your fault."

Grace gasped at Arie's words as Damien let out a low growl, grabbing Grace's hand once more.

"This has nothing to do with her, Arie," he said, wishing his brother would leave, although he supposed this was his own house. "That's enough."

"Very well," Arie said breezily. "I suppose I am just still a bit annoyed from the visit with her father, but all's well that ends well, or so they say, hmm?"

"You—you saw my father?" Grace said, wincing slightly, which Damien understood as he could also imagine how poorly that conversation had likely gone. "What happened?"

"Might as well take a seat," Arie said, gesturing to the bed, and Damien reached out an arm, drawing Grace into the small circle between his torso and his knees. He longed to truly take her into his arms, but he didn't seem to have the ability to do so at the moment.

Arie crossed his arms, eyebrows raised as he looked at

them. "Your father and I have come to an understanding. Thanks to Damien here."

"Arie, I didn't mean for the package—"

"It doesn't matter," Arie said, astonishing him by waving his hand in the air as though it was nothing. "As a matter of fact, I was actually rather proud of you."

"What?"

"Well, to go to such extremes is something only I would do! I could hardly believe you went that far, but I did admire it. I went to see Mulberry to threaten him back, but in the end, we worked out our differences and decided that, perhaps, it would be best to work together."

"You've got to be jesting," Grace said, her eyes wide and her face nearly unmoving as she stared at Arie as though she didn't believe a word he was saying.

Arie shrugged. "It's true. You can ask him when you return home. So that is settled — you do not have to worry about creating a new life for yourselves, Damien, because the only way Mulberry agreed to it all was if you were the one in the middle, working between us."

"Me?"

"You. The two of you are the common thread tying us together. Without you, this will never work."

Grace looked back at Damien, her mouth open in shock. Damien tried to shrug his shoulders but couldn't properly complete the gesture.

"I suppose we will all have to meet to determine the best way forward," he said cautiously. "If this is what we truly decide will work and will benefit everyone. After everything you've done Arie, I just don't know if we can trust you."

Damien honestly didn't know entirely what to think. Arie had been so adamant that he would never work with the man... what had changed so suddenly? And why should he believe his brother now?

"I can see why you might be sore," Arie said gruffly. "I thought I was doing what was best for the family, Damien, I did. But if this is what you truly want," he waved his hand forward toward Grace, as though encompassing all of Damien's wants and desires in her — which was, actually, as close to the truth as he could possibly come — "then I would rather that than lose you as a brother."

Damien was silent for a moment before he finally said what he was thinking — something he wasn't sure how Arie would react to, but it needed to be said anyway.

"You know this is becoming a pattern for you."

"What's that now?"

"Having to make amends to your siblings for trying to sabotage their happiness. I know Calli and Xander forgave you rather easily, but Arie… you *betrayed* me. After everything we've been through."

"I know," Arie said gruffly. "I suppose I just have a hard time understanding how a new love for someone else can come before your family. But I'm beginning to realize that while I may not understand it… I better start accepting it, for you lot are giving me no other choice."

Damien closed his eyes for a moment, needing to continue this conversation but also becoming rather fatigued following the range of emotions.

"I hope, Arie, that someday you will understand. That you will find that person who can make you do so."

"Likely not."

Damien knew there was more behind those words, more that Arie wasn't saying, but he didn't have the strength to push him any further. It would have to wait for another day.

Grace covered his hand with hers as she looked up at his brother.

"It is a nice gesture, Arie," she said, although there was hesitation in her words. "Thank you. If both my father and

Damien can forgive you, then I suppose I can too. I just finished a bit of grovelling myself."

Damien heard her words turn toward him, and he opened his eyes to meet her smile.

He knew that he was, in the end, a lucky man. A very lucky man indeed.

* * *

"GRACIE."

Grace looked up sharply when she stepped through the doorway of her parents' home, not expecting to hear her father's voice, as he was usually at his warehouse by now.

"Father?"

"Were you with Hondros?"

She didn't ask him which Hondros, as technically, she had seen both of them.

"Yes."

"I had an interesting visitor earlier today."

"I heard."

"Perhaps you best come in and sit down in my study."

And so her father told her all that Arie did, but surprised her by saying that while he didn't trust him, he was willing to tentatively agree to his plan, on two conditions.

"After everything that has happened, and everything that Damien was willing to do, I know that he always had our best interests at heart — certainly your interests, if nothing else. If he is involved to broker the deal, I am willing to go ahead. But at the first sign of trouble, I will use the information I now have to take them all down."

"About that..." Grace said, cringing slightly, wishing that Damien was here to offer for her hand but knew that was likely physically impossible at the moment. She took a deep breath. "Damien has asked me to marry him."

Her father was silent for a moment, staring at her over steepled fingers.

"Marry you," he finally repeated, showing no other sign of what he was thinking.

"Yes," she said, finding the courage to forge on. "He would ask you himself, but he sustained some fairly major injuries during a skirmish — one in which he was protecting me. He will likely be bedridden for a week or so as he recovers, but then I'm sure we can continue forward."

Another voice, unbidden, joined the conversation.

"Did I hear you mention marriage?"

Grace blinked. For a woman who often missed much of what occurred around her, her mother's ears seemed to pick up on certain topics of conversation, wherever they might be had in her house — topics including, apparently, marriage.

"Y-yes," Grace said. "Damien wishes to marry me."

"Oh, how wonderful!" her mother said, apparently forgetting all of the misdeeds she had previously been so distraught about if it meant that someone was going to marry her daughter. "Two weddings!"

"Two?" Grace said, wrinkling her nose in confusion.

"Oh, yes," her mother said, her hands underneath her chin, her fingers locked together. She looked to her husband. "Didn't you tell her?"

"I haven't had the chance."

"Borden asked Lydia for her hand in marriage just this morning."

"What!?" Grace exclaimed, getting to her feet. "How did I not know this?"

"Well, she didn't know of your news yet either," her mother said with a shrug. "Perhaps you best go speak to her."

"Perhaps I shall," Grace said, her mind still racing at a dizzying pace after all that had occurred in such a short time. "Thank you, Mother, Father — for everything!"

As it turned out, she didn't have far to go, for Lydia was already racing up the stairs to her house when Grace walked outside.

They both shared a smile of joy before embracing one another, laughing with incredulity at it all.

After all that had happened with Damien, she could hardly believe how everything had turned out. But, provided that he would recover without issue, it had been a good day. A good day indeed.

* * *

DAMIEN HAD BEEN SO worried that once Grace saw the extent of his injuries, knew they were the result of a fight, and that he had sustained them in following her, she would never want to see him again.

But fortune had smiled down on him, and now she had spent every moment over the past couple of weeks with him — well, the moments when she was not working at the bookshop. He had promised her that he would support her for the rest of her life, but she had been adamant that she could most use his support in understanding that she enjoyed her work and wanted to continue.

To that, he agreed. He couldn't help but agree. He would do anything for her.

As it was, the Hondros family wasn't much for following propriety. But given the circumstances, there had never been a question that Grace was welcome in his bedchamber alone or not.

The stronger Damien became, the more he had used that time to their advantage. Grace had been thrilled with his advances.

Today, he had a surprise for her.

When she walked into the room, he was standing, dressed, and leaning against the wardrobe.

"Damien!" she exclaimed when she walked in, and he grinned at the smile that lit her face. He would never tire of that smile — especially when he had put it there. "You look well today."

"I *feel* well today," he said, taking another look in the oval mirror in the corner of the room, one he didn't consult overly often. "I think the ribs are beginning to heal. Must have just been bruised, for if they had been broken, I still don't think I would be able to walk."

"It looks like you are walking just fine," she said, her eyes widening with every step toward her that he took.

"Oh, yes," he said. "I believe I am ready to resume my regular activities."

"Fighting?" she asked, looking up at him from beneath her lashes.

"No scheduled fighting," he said, shaking his head before taking a breath, needing her to understand how important this next part was. "Grace, I know for so long that this has been who I am, but I need you to know that I can be more than that. I promise, no more fighting. I will—"

"You don't have to change anything for me," she began, but he placed a finger against her lips.

"I want to do this," he said. "I don't enjoy it. I only fight when I must."

She nodded slowly before beginning to nibble her lip in a way that shot a rush down to his already growing organ. "So… what activities are you resuming, then?"

"Well," he said in a low voice, tilting his head down so that his forehead rested against hers. "I have a wife to please."

"A wife? Already? I think you forgot to mention her," Grace said, feigning annoyance, and Damien laughed.

"Very well. A wife in my heart, and soon to be in name through the church. How is that?"

"Much better."

"Good. Now come here, and I'll give you a little preview."

Before Grace could respond, he had lifted her up so that her legs were wrapped around his waist, his hands below her buttocks. His arousal was pressing into her, and he was pleased when, instead of moving away from him, Grace moaned and rubbed against him. So she wanted him as much as he wanted her. Good.

Damien knew he should likely wait again until their marriage, but he had meant what he said when he told her that he felt married in their hearts. He would show her what wedding him would mean, and just how much he truly loved her.

While his heart raced, pumping desire through his veins, Damien managed to set Grace down gently on the bed before lifting her skirts, rustling them up around her waist. Thank goodness Grace embraced the simple style of the day — he would use that to his advantage in the future. As it was, he had no time for undoing all of her buttons followed by removing layer after layer. No, he was going to go right for what he yearned for.

Damien looked up at her wide eyes, her flushed cheeks, the strands of hair that were already falling around her face. Then he grinned, and when she opened her mouth to tell him no, he simply shook his head, then disappeared under her skirts so that she couldn't say anything anymore.

As much as his body was telling him to hurry so that he could find his own relief, Damien took his time with her, making love to her with his mouth, finding that it only fueled his own desire, but he didn't care. All that mattered was that she understood just how great would be the pleasure she could reach.

And, from her keening cry, she reached fairly high.

When she finally came, pulsing around his fingers and against his lips, he lifted himself up, unfastened the fall of his breeches, and slid into her, to the place he was meant to be, finding home.

As he moved with her, his eyes met hers, locking in mutual understanding and commitment. And he knew then that no matter what else would come their way, everything would be all right.

For they would be together.

The very thought caused him to come within her with a ferocity he didn't know was possible, and as his blood pumped hard and fast and his body shook with the aftermath, he reached down and grasped her hand before leaning over and placing his lips against hers, in the promise of forever.

EPILOGUE

If Grace had one fault as a bookshop clerk and librarian, it was the fact that she sometimes became so distracted by the task at hand that she forgot to keep an ear out for whoever was approaching the desk for her help.

One of her colleagues, the very man who had done everything to dissuade her from applying, had noted it many times. She had been so praised by patrons and justified by her work, however, that in the end, she had won out as she found her own shifts increasing and her colleague's decreasing until he quit altogether.

Grace hadn't been able to help her little moment of triumph.

"I said excuse me, Miss."

Grace's heart fluttered as that familiar voice caused her to look up with a smile.

"My apologies, sir. May I help you with something?"

"As a matter of fact, you may," he said, not caring about who was watching them as he reached over and shut the book in front of her — although not before placing a mark in it so that she wouldn't lose her page. She was fortunate that he was so considerate — especially when it came to her books. "I need some help finding something."

"Of course, that's what I'm here for," she said, rising and rounding the desk. "What book is it?"

He leaned in, his breath tickling her neck beneath her ear. "Can I tell you a secret?"

She could only nod as her breath caught in her throat.

"It's a romance. A love story. Between a fighter and a woman who never gave up on him."

"I don't know that's how it truly went," she said, but he held up a finger.

"That's the synopsis," he said with a half-smile. "Perhaps you could help me find something along those lines."

"Very well."

"I have but one request."

"Which is?"

"We must begin our search in the farthest corner of the reading room — one which is rather deserted."

"That's very forward of you, sir," Grace said, even though she couldn't help stepping even closer to him.

"Just for a minute or two," he said with a wink, and she nodded slowly before leading him through the reading room, which was already beginning to empty as the closing hour approached.

Grace stepped toward a bookshelf that was hidden from view from the rest of the room, but before she could turn around to say anything, she found thick arms trapping her against the shelf and warm breath against her ear.

"This is more like it."

"Damien!" Grace gasped as she turned around, concerned about her reputation and yet equally thrilled by him. "We really shouldn't be doing this here."

"No, we shouldn't," he agreed, before bending his head

and kissing her lightly on the lips. "And I won't put your job in jeopardy. I promise. I just wanted you to know I was missing you."

Grace smiled, still amazed at how her life had turned out — with this man, who had been the man of her dreams, and now the man of her heart.

"I missed you too." She stroked his cheek. "How was your day?"

"It was… interesting," he said, leaning back from her, and tucking an errant strand of hair behind her ear. "My brother likes to make things difficult, but at the end of the day, he and your father have one similar interest."

"Making money?" Grace asked, raising an eyebrow.

"Correct. But at least they're all working together."

"Because of you."

He winked at her. "Well, wife, I will wait for you while you finish up. Do you have any books to recommend?"

"A romance?" she asked, cheekily.

"Of course."

"I have just the one."

She smiled impishly at him as she pulled one off the shelf. She hadn't just chosen this spot randomly — she had known he would enjoy this one.

"Here you are, sir."

"Thank you, Miss."

"It's Missus."

Grace looked around to ensure no one was looking, then leaned in and kissed him soundly.

"What was that for?" Damien asked.

"For being you," she said. "Enjoy your book."

"I will," he promised. "But there is one thing for certain."

"What's that?"

"I'll never find a completely satisfying happily ever after."

"Whyever not?"

"Because no other will ever be better than our own."

She smiled. "On that," she said, "you are right."

They began to walk back toward the entrance when Arie ran in, looking around the room frantically.

Damien took Grace's hand and rushed toward the entrance.

"Arie? What is it?"

"It's Diana," he said, his eyes wild. "She's gone."

THE END

* * *

Dear reader,

I hope you enjoyed reading Damien and Grace's story! Will Damien's sister, Diana, find a man who can match her? You can preview the first chapter of her story in the pages just after this one, or find it on Amazon here: Gambling for the Lost Lord's Love.

I would love to stay in touch with you! You can sign up for my newsletter today and "Unmasking a Duke," a regency romance, will come straight to your inbox — free!

www.elliestclair.com/ellies-newsletter

You will also receive links to giveaways, sales, updates, launch information, promos, and the newest recommended reads.

Or you can join my Facebook group, Ellie St. Clair's Ever Afters, and stay in touch daily.

Happy reading!

* * *

Gambling for the Lost Lord's Love
Thieves of Desire Book 4

If there was ever a forbidden love, this was it. John Wade. The very man who threatened to destroy all that Diana's family had ever built.

But by the time Diana realizes the man she has fallen for at the race track is the very man she has vowed to bring down, it is too late -- she's already lost her heart. And her hand in marriage.

Wade had said he'd needed a wife. He just hadn't counted on falling for the sister of his greatest foe. For Wade is trying to build his own empire, to become a man who is as feared and respected as Arie Hondros. And he must do so while facing secrets from the past he never saw coming -- secrets that question everything he ever knew about himself.

The trust between Diana and Wade is as shallow as their passion for one another is deep. But when a shadowy figure from their pasts threatens all that they know and all who they love, they must learn to work together or risk losing everything -- including each other.

AN EXCERPT FROM GAMBLING FOR THE LOST LORD'S LOVE

CHAPTER ONE (ONE WEEK EARLIER)

Diana stood at the entrance of the room, arms crossed over her chest as she allowed the corners of her mouth to turn up in a small outward gesture of satisfaction. The coins and notes flipped between fingers, one after another, as mouths silently counted before pens were dipped in ink and then scratched onto the ledgers in front of them.

It was a good day – which was to be expected, what with the upcoming race just outside of London and the talk they had created regarding the horse that was supposed to win.

The horse that *would* win, if Arie had anything to do with it.

It was also collection day, and as far as Diana knew, everyone had fallen in line as expected.

Hearing footsteps above her, she knew that the men and women who were legally employed by them – the Hondros family – must have begun to prepare for the night ahead in the gambling hell, and she turned around to head upstairs to ensure all was in order.

She stopped short when she found her brother, Arie, behind her.

"There you are."

"Where else would I be?" she quirked an eyebrow as she brushed around him. She had no time to chit chat. There was far too much to do, especially now that most of their siblings had left the family business for other priorities they deemed far more important.

"You weren't at home earlier."

"No. Today is collection day, in case you forgot."

"Of course I didn't forget," Arie said, keeping up with her slow, measured stride, which allowed her to ensure that all around her was in order – the clean hallway, the polished banister as they followed the stairs up. They continued in silence down the corridor, moving as one. They had worked together for so many years now that they didn't need to even discuss what needed to be done.

Diana paused at the threshold of the hell, casting her gaze over the room. The floors had already been cleaned, as evidenced by the smell of lemon and vinegar that washed over them. Roland, one of the barmen, was standing on a ladder, lighting the candles of the chandelier as the light from the windows was beginning to wan. Men and women – the card dealers and the barmaids – began to push the tables in toward the centre of the room, arranging the chairs around them as they set up their games of faro, whist, vingt-un, and other games of chance.

All here had to be above board, so that they wouldn't be caught doing what they did below.

"We need more hires," Diana said quietly to Arie, who turned to her sharply.

"Why?"

"We've taken on so much more and we no longer have Xander and Calli helping us. I know Damien is overlooking the business with Mulberry, but there is so much product to be moved."

Arie said nothing, his only response the slight flare of his nostrils as he looked around the room. He kept all of his interests under careful control, not allowing anything to be out of place.

"It will cost us."

"Of course it will. But we are also bringing in more than we ever have before."

He gave a short, curt nod.

"What do you suggest?"

Diana couldn't help the slight thrill that he cared about what he thought, that he appreciated her competency, at least in this regard.

"We need to hire more women to help with the accounting and the books below."

"Women?" He arched a heavy brow as he turned to her.

"Yes," she said, nodding. "They are far more loyal. Too many men have left us as of late."

Arie stayed silent once more, although Diana could sense the tenseness of his shoulders as he slightly turned toward her.

"It's the Bronze Reapers."

"It is," Diana said, not allowing Arie to see how she truly felt. For there was more past with the gang than just their sudden determination to strip the Hondros clan of all of their endeavours.

"I don't understand how they've amassed such a following as of late. Have you heard anything?"

She had. Diana always made sure that she knew everything there was to know on the streets of London – particularly on these very streets of St. Giles. Anything regarding this particular gang always caused a great deal of discord within her, however. She felt the twitch of her eye and hoped Arie didn't notice as she kept her hands firmly clasped behind her back, above the dark, linen fabric of her skirt.

"I'm told they have a new leader."

"What?" That caught Arie's attention, and he turned to her abruptly. "How do I not know about this?"

"It's unofficial," she said, unaffected by Arie's chagrin. He always had a great deal of anger directed to someone, and one had to stand up to him in order to not be taken advantage of. "Gibson has, apparently, disappeared."

She took a breath to steady the beating of her heart, as she had to whenever the man's name was mentioned – particularly when it came out of her own mouth. She closed her eyes for a moment to rid herself the thought of what her life would be like if she was still with the Bronze Reapers, if Arie hadn't rescued her that one fateful night.

"Who is in charge?" Arie asked, his eyes narrowing at her, although Diana was aware that he already knew.

"A man named Wade."

"Wade," Arie seethed, the man's name leaking through his teeth in a hiss. "Of course. Bloody hell."

"I know," Diana said quietly, although it was one name that had no affect on her. She had never met him. She had heard much about him, of course. One couldn't live the life she did without knowing more about the man who was one of the most well known in all of St. Giles besides her own brothers.

Unlike Arie, however, Wade was apparently also well-liked.

Of course, he didn't frequent the Hondros establishment, and Diana would never venture to another. If she passed him on the street, she would have continued on, not even knowing what he looked like.

"When the men went around to collect today, there were two businesses who have chosen to change their alliance. They have committed to The Bronze Reapers instead."

"Who?" Arie asked through clenched teeth.

"The Crown and Hand and O'Hanley's on the corner."

"I will speak to them tomorrow."

Diana swallowed, unsure of just exactly what Arie meant by *speaking* to them, but that was an aspect of the business she chose not to become involved in.

"Very well. There is also the horse race tomorrow."

"I know. That should take care of itself now. We need to get to the bottom of this… issue before we lose control."

"I agree," she said, turning her eyes on her brother, who to anyone else may have seemed composed, but she was well aware that there was a storm brewing within him. "Just what do you propose?"

~~~~~

WADE LEANED BACK and stretched his arms out over the sides of the sofa.

Well, if one could call it a sofa.

It was slightly dilapidated and had seen better days – as had most of this building.

But he was going to change all of that.

"Tell me, Edward, what do you have for me?"

He crossed one leg over the other as he considered his man in front of him. He was as close as a brother would be, if not more so, and the only man in the world that Wade trusted.

"Twas a good day," Edward said, slapping his hat on his
~~~~~

knee. "The Crown and Hand and O'Hanley's both paid up quick, 'specially after you cut their rate in half."

"For double the protection," Wade couldn't help but boast, just as he had when he had convinced the owners to defect to him.

"Right. Should be more, now that 'tis known protection's on offer by more than just one."

"And you, Tiger, do you have anything to share with us?" He smiled as warmly as he could at the boy. Only about eleven years, he had seen more than his fair share in his lifetime. Working for Gibson did that to a person. Wade would know.

"Hondros' men were none too happy when they went to collect, sir," Tiger said, his speech beginning to quicken as he seemed eager to share what he knew, his hesitancy being overcome by his intent to show his usefulness. "Never saw the man meself, though."

"Of course not," Wade muttered. "He sits on his throne while he waits for all of his men to do the work for him."

"And women," Tiger added helpfully. "'es got many women on pay too, I'm told."

"Doing what?" Wade asked, leaning forward as his elbows came to his knees, and he took a moment to admire the trousers he had bought for himself once he took over control.

"None too sure, exactly," Tiger said, scratching his head, and his cap fell off and to the floor. Edward picked it up for him, the boy gripping it tightly between his fingers when he took it back. "But not just as barmaids and whores and the like."

"I see," Wade said, rolling his shoulders to get rid of the tension that built up at this point in time, when he felt the weight of all the people who depended on him now descending onto him. "Interesting."

He had a plan. One that included slowly, carefully, taking down Arie Hondros one block at a time.

He and Hondros had a past. They had known one another as well as any two young men could. But then everything had changed.

The Hondros family had maintained total control of St. Giles for long enough. Sure, Gibson was known and feared, but he wasn't respected, not like Hondros. Gibson was a brute, one who took advantage of those who worked for him, who made life hell for the men and women under his control.

But he was seen as the scum of the earth he was, and had taken the entire Bronze Reaper organization along with him.

Wade was going to change that.

"Tomorrow's race day," Edward added helpfully. "We've a few bets going, although most have picked up on the chatter about Charmed. Queen Calico should have been the true winner, but…"

"But Hondros has something cooking," Wade finished, his mouth set in a grim line. "We shall see about that. Have our people bet on Queen Calico. And have them bet at Aphrodite's."

Edward's shifted uncomfortable in his seat. "But that's Hondros' establishment."

"It is."

"The betting there is illegal."

"And what we do is legal?" Wade asked, spreading his hands out before him. "That's not what I'm after, Edward."

"You want to win the money back from Hondros," Tiger said, his eyes gleaming excitedly as he leaned forward so far that he fell out of his seat.

Wade reached out a hand and caught him.

"The young one understands."

"But—"

"We are going to make sure that Hondros doesn't fix that horse race tomorrow," Wade said, standing now and crossing his arms over his chest as he began to pace from one side of the room to the other. "We will have all of our men there, and we will stop him before he can do whatever he is going to do to sabotage that race. Edward, you will stay with Queen Calico at all times."

"I don't think—"

"Disguise yourself as a groom, get into the stables, I don't care what you do, but you will do it. Understand?"

Wade knew it was best to capture affection and acquiescence with charm, but he didn't appreciate when someone disagreed with him. Especially when he knew he was right.

"Understood," Edward muttered.

"Good." Wade smiled grimly in satisfaction. "We are going to show Hondros just who is in charge now."

* * *

Wondering what will happen between Diana and Wade? Keep reading Gambling for the Lost Lord's Love.

ALSO BY ELLIE ST. CLAIR

Thieves of Desire

The Art of Stealing a Duke's Heart

A Jewel for the Taking

A Prize Worth Fighting For

Gambling for the Lost Lord's Love

Romance of a Robbery

Thieves of Desire Box Set

Reckless Rogues

The Earls's Secret

The Viscount's Code

The Scholar's Key

Prequel, The Duke's Treasure, available in:

I Like Big Dukes and I Cannot Lie

The Remingtons of the Regency

The Mystery of the Debonair Duke

The Secret of the Dashing Detective

The Clue of the Brilliant Bastard

The Quest of the Reclusive Rogue

The Unconventional Ladies

Lady of Mystery

Lady of Fortune

Lady of Providence

Lady of Charade

The Unconventional Ladies Box Set

To the Time of the Highlanders

A Time to Wed

A Time to Love

A Time to Dream

The Bluestocking Scandals

Designs on a Duke

Inventing the Viscount

Discovering the Baron

The Valet Experiment

Writing the Rake

Risking the Detective

A Noble Excavation

A Gentleman of Mystery

The Bluestocking Scandals Box Set: Books 1-4

The Bluestocking Scandals Box Set: Books 5-8

Blooming Brides

A Duke for Daisy

A Marquess for Marigold

An Earl for Iris

A Viscount for Violet

The Blooming Brides Box Set: Books 1-4

Happily Ever After

The Duke She Wished For

Someday Her Duke Will Come

Once Upon a Duke's Dream

He's a Duke, But I Love Him

Loved by the Viscount

Because the Earl Loved Me

Happily Ever After Box Set Books 1-3

Happily Ever After Box Set Books 4-6

The Victorian Highlanders

Duncan's Christmas - (prequel)

Callum's Vow

Finlay's Duty

Adam's Call

Roderick's Purpose

Peggy's Love

The Victorian Highlanders Box Set Books 1-5

Searching Hearts

Duke of Christmas (prequel)

Quest of Honor

Clue of Affection

Hearts of Trust

Hope of Romance

Promise of Redemption

Searching Hearts Box Set (Books 1-5)

Christmas

Christmastide with His Countess

Her Christmas Wish

Merry Misrule

A Match Made at Christmas

A Match Made in Winter

Standalones

Always Your Love

The Stormswept Stowaway

A Touch of Temptation

For a full list of all of Ellie's books, please see

www.elliestclair.com/books.

ABOUT THE AUTHOR

Ellie has always loved reading, writing, and history. For many years she has written short stories, non-fiction, and has worked on her true love and passion -- romance novels.

In every era there is the chance for romance, and Ellie enjoys exploring many different time periods, cultures, and geographic locations. No matter when or where, love can always prevail. She has a particular soft spot for the bad boys of history, and loves a strong heroine in her stories.

Ellie and her husband love nothing more than spending time at home with their children and Husky cross. Ellie can typically be found at the lake in the summer, pushing the stroller all year round, and, of course, with her computer in her lap or a book in hand.

She also loves corresponding with readers, so be sure to contact her!

www.elliestclair.com
ellie@elliestclair.com

Ellie St. Clair's Ever Afters Facebook Group

Made in the USA
Monee, IL
09 April 2024

56641128R00152